ASHLEY BEEGAN

The Hospital

Copyright © 2022 by Ashley Beegan

All rights reserved. No part of this publication may be reproduced, stored or transmitted in any form or by any means, electronic, mechanical, photocopying, recording, scanning, or otherwise without written permission from the publisher. It is illegal to copy this book, post it to a website, or distribute it by any other means without permission.

This novel is entirely a work of fiction. The names, characters and incidents portrayed in it are the work of the author's imagination. Any resemblance to actual persons, living or dead, events or localities is entirely coincidental.

Ashley Beegan asserts the moral right to be identified as the author of this work.

First edition

Cover art by Black Cat Design
Editing by Starlight Book Editing

This book was professionally typeset on Reedsy.
Find out more at reedsy.com

*Dedicated to one funny ass bitch, Ellie Owen.
Thank you for reading my terrible, unedited drafts and still being so amazing and supportive!*

Contents

1	The Servant	1
2	Swanson	7
3	Summer	14
4	The Servant	23
5	Swanson	26
6	Summer	29
7	Swanson	34
8	Summer	36
9	The Servant	46
10	Swanson	50
11	The Servant	58
12	Swanson	60
13	The Servant	64
14	Swanson	67
15	Swanson	81
16	Swanson	89
17	The Servant	95
18	Swanson	97
19	Swanson	105
20	Swanson	110
21	Swanson	117
22	The Servant	124
23	Swanson	126
24	Swanson	134

25	Summer	139
26	Swanson	146
27	Swanson	153
28	Swanson	160
29	Swanson	164
30	The Servant	169
31	Swanson	173
32	The Servant	176
33	Swanson	178
34	Summer	183
35	The Servant	187
36	Swanson	190
37	Summer	195
38	The Servant	197
39	Swanson	200
40	Swanson	204
41	Swanson	208
42	The Servant	213
43	Swanson	220
44	Swanson	225
45	Swanson	230
46	Summer	232
Also by Ashley Beegan		235

1

The Servant

The freezing breeze numbed the tip of my nose as I waited outside Derby Psychiatric Hospital, reminding me to pull up the thick scarf to hide the bottom half of my face. I made sure only my eyes were visible and pulled my hood further forward to block out the wind, though it still whirled around me, as if pushing me away from my dark calling. Every few minutes, a member of staff arrived in the car park. They yawned and stretched as they mentally prepared to begin their 6am shift.

But they didn't concern me.

Despite being over six feet tall, the prickly branches belonging to a smattering of unkempt bushes hid me well; opposite from the hospital car park. I was lucky it was the depths of winter, and the dark sky would stay that way for another couple of hours.

My cheeks flushed under the warmth of the scarf, and a tingle of anticipation ran through my skin. This was the day.

No more watching. No more waiting.

I knew Derby Psychiatric Hospital well from my stint there

a few years back. The door I was staring at was the only exit and entry point that was used. A couple of fire exits allowed patients into the rear gardens for walking or smoking, but this was the staff door. The bushes were an excellent choice to watch the doors without being seen. I watched the staff come and go easily.

There was no way I could miss her.

The wind flew straight through the small holes in the cheap soles of my Chelsea boots. I moved from one foot to the other to prevent my feet from going numb, though it helped as the minutes slipped by, and nerves replaced my excitement.

I checked the silver face of the Rolex my father gifted to me years ago. It was 6:10am. The date was definitely the 1st of December. I was certain I had the right day. She needed to hurry. Time was not on my side.

He would not wait another day.

Why was she late today of all days?

I stopped moving and reached deep into the fleece-lined pocket of my hiking jacket. My fingers curled around the hard shape of an A5-sized notepad. The front cover emblazoned with 'Adrenna Hospital' in small white letters. I flicked through the last few pages, looking for any errors.

Wednesday November 24th

She worked the night shift. Arrived at 5:35pm and left at 6:09am.

Thursday November 25th

She worked the night shift. Arrived at 5:46pm and left at 6:11am.

Friday November 26th

She worked the night shift. Arrived at 5:43pm and left at 6:10am.

No errors. I definitely had the right day. She worked on Wednesday every week, and it was now 6:14am. Being tardy wouldn't do.

Maybe she wasn't even the right one for Him.

I chewed my lip and considered the reaction if I was to give him the wrong woman. *Was it worth the risk?*

The whirring noise of the doors opening made my head snap back up. And finally, there she was. She bolted through the hospital doors with her head high in the air, missing the usual exhausted look of someone finishing a night shift. She never seemed to look tired.

Though she gave a slight shiver as she crossed the road and pulled her dark winter coat firmly around her. I stayed well back, but wondered why she didn't zip it up.

I pushed away my doubts. She was the one. I felt it. Though at first glance there was nothing special about the young woman in her everyday blue jeans and plain brown boots. It was all in her haughty demeanour. Her narrow eyes. She needed to be tamed. And He was the one to do it.

She had a proud walk as she made her way down the long pavements of London Road. I followed a suitable distance behind as we passed closed shops, old cafes, and Indian restaurants. Long blonde hair peeked out of her woolly bobble hat. I wanted to get closer, to touch it, to see how soft it was. But I forced myself to stay back.

A cotton scarf sat a little too tightly around her neck. She clearly wore it for decoration only, as it was too thin to be keeping anything warm against the cool winter temperatures.

I'd definitely gotten it right this time. I only needed to get the hard part over with and then I'd rest. The thought of sleep kept me moving, hands in pockets, tracing her footsteps as she continued down the last half a mile of London Road which led to the bus station.

I didn't rush. I didn't need to keep up because I knew where she was heading. She used the same route each time to get home after her regular shift at the hospital.

Though my legs were longer than hers, and so I accidentally caught up with her seconds before she reached the roundabout across from a large shopping complex and city centre market, which stood proudly on the edge of the cobbled city centre. She stood at the roadside and craned her neck, looking for cars coming from either direction.

This was my chance.

I pulled my scarf down and ran forward, spat on my hands and rubbed my eyes hard.

"Excuse me!" I yelled, my voice high and panicked.

Her head whipped around, dark eyes wide against pale skin.

"Please! Can you help me? It's my mother." I pointed to the car park of the kids' indoor trampoline play park, which sat behind us.

She stepped forward, but hesitated and looked around at the empty streets behind her.

"What's wrong with her?" She turned back to face me, and her face creased with worry. Though she didn't move any closer.

I'd have to try harder.

I scrunched up my nose as if holding back tears and shrugged my shoulders. "She just collapsed."

The woman took another look around. The streets were silent.

I could run at her.

"OK. It's OK, don't worry. I'm a nurse." She finally moved towards me and relief flooded me.

"Oh, thank you!" I turned and ran toward the secluded car park of the trampoline place. It was the only car park I found nearby which had no cameras.

She followed closely behind me and we ran to the road behind the shopping centre, pausing a moment and checking for traffic. It was strange, being so close to her after keeping my distance for so long. I breathed in the sweet smell of her perfume. Or was it shampoo? It was something flowery.

It was my favourite smell in a woman, and I hadn't expected it from her. A longing to touch her almost took over me, but I kept my hands firmly at my side and squeezed into fists.

It wasn't time yet.

And she wasn't mine to have.

One car drove by. A taxi. I put my head down as it passed, hoping my hood and scarf were enough to hide my face. But my concern was unfounded. The taxi driver was going far too fast to see anything much. I ran across the road once it had passed, and she followed right behind me.

"Over here." I led her to the side of the car park where I'd parked the large van earlier that morning.

She stopped on the other side of the van. *Damn.* She was still visible to the road.

I disappeared around the side of the van and stood with my back to it. I reached into my pocket, my fist tightening around the needle that lay hidden inside it.

"Mum? Can you hear me?" My voice came out strangled, and my heart quickened as I heard her boots getting closer to my side of the van. I stood firm, took a deep breath.

I saw the toe of her brown boot first and a flash of blonde hair a second later. I grabbed her hair and pulled her towards me. She cried out, her hands grabbed at mine.

Until I smashed her head against the van.

Her body went limp, and I plunged the syringe into her neck.

In an instant, it was over, and she lay on the ground, motionless. I peered around the other side of the van. No one was there. No one came running. Opening up the rear doors of the van, I dragged her by her feet and hauled her into the back. There was no need to be careful. She wouldn't wake for a while.

I climbed into the van and closed the door. I removed her shoes and woolly hat and put the faint scarf to one side. Her hair fell over her face, and I brushed it back. For the first time, I noticed the dark makeup around her eyes and tutted. I'd smudged it in the brief struggle. I'd have to remove it before He saw her.

I stripped the rest of her body, carefully placing her underwear into my pocket and the scarf back around her neck. I pulled it tight. Not enough to cut off her air supply. But enough that it wouldn't be hard to calm her in case it had to be over with quickly.

Once naked, I lay her on her back and stared. I wasn't supposed to touch her, but thinking about the way she walked, that narrow look in her eyes, and seeing her now.

She was helpless.

And it occurred to me it would solve my problem of whether she was good enough to be taken for Him. I'd *humble* her before He got to her. I had to make sure she knew her place. That was the answer to our minor problem.

I lay a finger on her shoulder. Her soft skin spoke to me. And I knew I was right.

This time, everything would be perfect. And I would make sure she was ready for her new beginning.

2

Swanson

The whiteness of the doctor's office closed in around Detective Inspector Alex Swanson. His breath stuck in his lungs. Why were the walls so bare? There was nothing to focus on. It was always the mundane things he noticed when in need of a distraction. Other people who had sat in this chair, and received the same news, might scream, or cry or swear.

Is that what he should do?

He stayed silent and tore his gaze away from the walls, focusing on the dulled floor tiles and trying to force air through his lungs again.

But the tiles weren't much help either, and his lungs ached to the point it was difficult to breathe. He needed to get out. It was too damn hot and stuffy in here, and the brightness was too much for his aching head. The room vibrated so hard around him he had to close his eyes and put his head in his hands to make it stop.

"Are you OK, Alex? Is there someone I can call for you?" Dr Nick Tiffin's voice rang through somehow. The city's top neurologist sounded far away and his voice echoed off the empty walls as if they were in a tunnel. Maybe they were in a tunnel, or even a dream, and none of this was real.

But Swanson rarely dreamed.

And if he did, why would he dream about cancer?

A hand on his shoulder broke his train of thought, and his head shot back up. Dr Tiffin had come out from behind his desk, and was bending over in front of Swanson, his large hand gripping his shoulder. Despite the man's considerable size, Swanson hadn't heard him coming. He ignored the deep throb in the base of his skull and stared at the dark five o'clock shadow on the doctor's chin.

"I'm fine. What are the next steps?" he heard himself say.

Dr Tiffin let go of his shoulder and walked back around to his side of the desk. He sat back in his chair, clasped his hands together, and eyed Swanson.

"Are you sure you don't need five minutes to yourself before we discuss this? It's a lot to take in," he said.

Swanson looked away and shifted in his chair, trying to make the dizziness stop. "I'm fine," he repeated.

"OK. Well, you need to be aware of the symptoms and what we can do to manage them. Headaches, nausea, even hallucinations can be possible, and you need to keep me informed. I know you've been having headaches of differing severity, so I'll prescribe some powerful painkillers and some mild ones. We need to figure out the type of tumour you have to determine the next steps, and in order to do that, we need to assess it. In the meantime, you can take these if you get any headaches." The doctor spoke slowly, and didn't take his eyes off Swanson once. He passed him a packet of pills.

Swanson reached over and grabbed them. The cheap plastic

chair groaned as he did so. "Thanks. How do we assess it?"

Dr Tiffin looked away, searching for something on his desk. Eventually, he opened a drawer and rummaged through it. "I'll refer you for a biopsy. Have you ever had one before?" He pulled out a pad of prescription paper and scribbled something down on it.

Swanson shook his head. "I've heard of them, but no, I've never needed one."

Dr Tiffin leaned over the desk and gave him a sympathetic smile as he handed over the torn piece of prescription paper. Swanson fought an urge to tell him to stop fucking smiling.

"It sounds scary, but it's actually quite a simple procedure and nothing to worry about. We'll make a small hole in the skull and insert a very fine needle to take a sample. It's done under anaesthetic, so you won't feel a thing."

Swanson's hand flew to the top of his head. A hole in his skull sounded like something to worry about to him.

"OK." Swanson stood. He couldn't stand the whiteness of the room any longer, or the patronising smile on the doctor's face. "You'll contact me with an appointment?"

"Er… yes." Dr Tiffin stood too. "But please, sit and I'll go through the options of the biopsy."

"Sorry, I have to go to work." Swanson turned and stalked out of the office without another word, ignoring Dr Tiffin's calls to come back.

His legs were shaky as he closed the office door firmly behind him and ventured into the rowdy corridor. The noise hit him immediately and seemed ten times louder than usual. Plastic chairs lined the walkway on one side. They were full of people muttering to their friends or partners, or with forlorn faces waiting to be called for their own appointments. Preoccupied hospital staff stalked through the corridor. Nurses, doctors, porters everywhere. Their sharp footsteps echoed off the floor and imprinted on Swanson's brain. He leant against the wall and closed his eyes, trying to drown out the noise.

"Are you OK, Sir?"

His eyes flew open. A young nurse stood in front of him, her head cocked to one side. A small smile lined her plump face, and her round eyes creased with worry. He cleared his throat, stood straight, and forced a smile.

"Yes, sorry. Just have a bit of a headache." He turned and strode off down the corridor. The nurse didn't follow, but he felt her eyes on his back as he walked away.

His legs marched rigidly through the winding corridors. Anyone in his way soon moved to the side to let him pass, one upside of being too broad to hide within a room. He reached the open reception area and fixated on the exit on the other side. The winter sun shone through the glass doors in front of him like a beacon.

He barely noticed the other patients sitting in the cheap waiting chairs, most of whom turned to look up at him as he rushed past. He vaguely noticed one older lady in a pale blue suit half stand up from her chair, as though she wanted to check on him, but he shot her a look which changed her mind and she swiftly plonked back down in her chair.

Reaching the automatic doors was all that mattered to him. As he finally stumbled through the doors and into the ambulance waiting area, he put his head to his hands. The sun was deceiving, and a freezing wind whipped at his face, forcing him to suck in a deep breath.

A mother and child steered clear of him as they tried to enter the hospital doors without getting too close. The mother clasped the hand of her little boy and pulled him close to her whilst they manoeuvred around Swanson.

He stepped away from the doors and leant against the external wall of the hospital instead. Unlike the more modern parts of the extended hospital, the original entrance was made of cold, red brick which dug into his shoulders. He moved his head back and let the brick dig in further. The pain helped. His thoughts became more focused.

Something sharp dug into his stomach and he shoved his hand into his pocket to move the item. The pills! He grabbed them and broke two tablets out. They were like dust in his mouth, but he forced himself to swallow them down.

Now he needed to get to his car.

He looked over at the car park and tried to remember where he had parked two hours ago. A vague memory of being annoyed at how busy the car park was came back to him. He'd driven right to the rear of the colossal car park to find a space where his Audi wasn't likely to get another car door slammed into the side of it.

He stepped forward to start the long walk. At least the freezing wind might clear his head before driving to the office. He looked down at the ground as he walked and ignored his surroundings. A couple of cars beeped at him as he got in their way, but he didn't bother looking up. Let them get annoyed.

They'd live.

He might not.

It took him fifteen minutes to find his car, and another couple more to find his keys. He eventually dug them out of the same pocket he'd looked in first, cursing at his carelessness. The wind made his nose and cheeks numb, but he was in no rush to drive away. The large saloon car suddenly felt too small to climb inside.

He unlocked the door and clenched his fists, took a few deep breaths and pulled the door open to force himself into the front seat. The air had woken him up enough to at least be thankful that no one else had parked next to him. There was never enough space in these tight bloody car parks.

The thought of work made him want to drive to the other side of the country and never return. He could go home, curl up, and pretend nothing was happening. Or he could get out into the fresh air some more. Maybe he should go to Mam Tor, a beautiful Derbyshire viewpoint that stretched over Edale Valley to Kinder Scout. There wouldn't be many people there in this awful weather. It was perfect.

He pulled his phone out of his pocket. Three missed calls flashed up from his most intense colleague, Detective Inspector Rebecca Hart.

No surprise there. She seemed to treat chasing him as her part-time job. But *three* were a lot of missed calls, even for Hart. Something must have happened. Damn it, why had he left his phone on silent? He started the engine and used the in-car phone system to call her back.

"Oh, here he is," she said. He practically heard her rolling her eyes. "It's about damn time you called me back, Swanson."

He'd never admit it, but hearing her voice dripping with sarcasm made his world still again. The beginnings of a grin formed on his lips for the first time that morning.

"Alright, Robin?" he replied in his usual calm manner.

"I'm warning you, Krypto. You are cruisin for a bruisin."

Krypto. Superman's loyal dog. He laughed softly. "Who even says cruisin for a bruisin anymore?"

She huffed. "All the cool kids do. Obviously."

"Well, you're showing your age with that one. What do you want, anyway? I'm busy." He stretched back in his seat and relaxed a little, allowing his eyes to wander around the car park. It seemed brighter suddenly, though the wind still howled.

"Busy going to the doctor for those damn headaches, I hope."

He sighed as she brought his reality back in an instant. "Yes, actually."

"Oh," Hart paused, momentarily thrown by his words. She'd been going on at him for weeks to go to the doctor, and he'd never told her he'd had a scan. He watched an old man walk past his car, bent over in the wind, and wondered if he would ever have the privilege of reaching such an age. He'd always looked forward to getting old. An age where you can do or say as you please and no one bats an eyelid because you're old. You can sit in pyjamas all day, shouting at the telly and smoking a pipe with no concerns about consequences when you're already 90.

"What did they say?" Hart's voice shook his thoughts away.

"I'm fine. I'm done now, so I'll see you in the office shortly," he said, and hung up before she replied. He grinned to himself, knowing she would spit feathers at him for cutting her off.

Maybe going into the office wouldn't be so bad, after all.

3

Summer

Summer Thomas cursed her brand new winter boots as she tripped over the curb outside the compact cafe nestled amongst the terraced street. She righted herself at the last minute, just in time to prevent a fall on her backside in the middle of the pavement. She'd known the boots were too big but could not resist the faux fur lining in the cool temperatures, especially at half-price.

She pushed away a piece of hair that had fallen out of place and into her face. Thank god it was only two more weeks until her hairdresser appointment. Although she hated the small talk and awkwardness of a stranger touching her hair, it had been *way* too long since she last had it cut. And now it had grown down to the middle of her back.

Dylan Thomas stood outside the entrance to the cafe watching her. He let out a short laugh.

"Did you enjoy your trip?" he asked, grinning widely.

Christ, she remembered kids at school saying that whenever anyone tripped up in the classroom. She finished sorting her hair and looked up at him, returning his grin. He might have been her younger brother, but he'd been taller than her since he was 13-years-old.

"How old are you? Ten?" she retorted.

"Not as old as you!" He grinned even wider, his bright white teeth almost glinting in the sun.

She tutted as she stepped forward to reach him. "You're only younger than me by two years! You'll be thirty soon and it won't matter. Age is just a number."

She pushed past him and opened the door to the cafe named 'Barbara's Baps'. The bell above the door jingled as she entered, and the greasy aroma of chips made her stomach rumble.

"Is that why you cried at your 30th birthday bash?" Dylan asked, following her through the open door.

"No. That was because of the prosecco."

She walked over to a table in front of the window and gestured for Dylan to sit across from her. The cafe was small, but it served tasty food that was freshly cooked, and it never got that busy. Perfect for a private conversation, and she wouldn't have to cook later because 6-year-old Joshua was at his dad's house for the night.

"So, what have you done to your teeth?" she asked as they removed their coats and took a seat on opposite sides of the table. A cheap, green and white plastic cloth in a chequered pattern covered the table. The same grim colour scheme as the external front, and the old aprons the servers wore.

He grinned widely and gritted his teeth. "Do you like them?" he asked. He moved his head to the left and the right, showing off all angles of his wide smile.

"Yeah, to be fair, they do look good. Maybe a bit *too* white. As in, I think I've gone blind." She leaned her elbows on the table, but jumped back as it tipped suddenly.

Dylan quit his stupid grin. "There's no such thing as *too* white. Watch the table. I see you're as clumsy as ever." He shook his head and picked up a menu.

Summer didn't bother to argue his point. She had always been clumsy. A waitress with wispy grey hair came out from behind the counter and approached them. She held a pen and a pad of paper tight in her thick fingers.

"What can I get for you?" She gave a half smile and looked out of the window.

"I'll have a cheese toastie, please," Summer said, not bothering to look at the menu.

"One cheese toastie." The waitress repeated as she wrote on her notepad. She squinted at the paper as she wrote, then looked up at Dylan expectantly.

"Er…" Dylan's eyes flicked over the menu. "Cheese and ham toastie, if that's on here somewhere?"

"Cheese and ham." The waitress nodded and peered down at her notepad again. "Any drinks?"

"Coke, please," said the pair simultaneously.

The waitress chuckled. "Coming right up." She turned and lumbered off back to the counter without another word.

"So, now I know you're OK, other than tripping over everything and breaking perfectly stable tables." He stopped for a moment and waited for her reaction with a cheeky glint in his eye. She rolled her eyes but said nothing. "Do you have any news about our lovely Eddie?"

She sighed. "No, nothing yet. I don't know what to do next, really. I replied to him on Facebook, but he didn't get my message. That police officer or detective, Alex Swanson, came with me to speak to a few of the homeless people in the city twice now, and no one has seen him. Or at least they didn't want to tell me. I don't have any pictures of him, so it wasn't easy. I called you thinking we'd brainstorm together."

Dylan nodded. "OK, but I have no idea where to even start, to be honest. I barely remember Eddie. I was what, 8 when he got locked up? And work is crazy busy. Everyone wants their carpets fitted before Christmas. I'm working 12-hour days, including most weekends."

"I know. I'm busy, too. But he's our brother regardless of whether we remember him well. I want to know he's safe and not dead in a ditch somewhere with no one to claim him." She sat back on the hard, plastic chair and shuffled a bit to stop her backside going numb.

"Or make sure he's not hurting anybody?" Dylan raised an eyebrow.

"Well, yes, or make sure he's not hurting anybody. But Aaron checked out his record from Adrenna Hospital, which is where he was for a good couple of years, and he was *never* violent there with staff or patients. I really don't think he's a danger to anyone anymore. Other than himself, possibly. He's been in hospitals for so long, how would he know how to look after himself without someone always being there?" Summer kept her voice low. They were discussing a fugitive, after all.

"Yes, true. But if he's off his medication, he might be more of a danger to others. As in, maybe that's what kept him calm?" Dylan suggested.

"He wouldn't have needed medication in the first place if Marinda hadn't messed with his head, pretending to be some sort of demon. He was never violent before her, or before Dad died."

Dylan looked away as soon as she mentioned their dad, and she instantly felt guilty for mentioning their father's death.

She'd only been 9-years-old when he passed and her memories of him were faint, but Dylan barely remembered him at all.

"Look, if they have medicated him for years for a mental disorder he doesn't actually have, he might actually be feeling a lot better *off* his meds." She tried to explain as Dylan didn't have the experience she had with mental illness.

"Oh, really? Is that what would happen?" Dylan turned back to look at her.

"Well, I'm not a doctor, but it sounds like a possibility to me. Those medications are so strong and have all sorts of side effects. They were literally made to mess with your brain. Doesn't it make sense to you that he would feel better off them? At least after the initial shock to his body." She leaned forward again, ignoring the tip of the table this time.

"I actually thought you *were* some sort of psychiatric doctor?" He squinted at her.

She tutted. "Why do you and Mum always say that? No. I'm *training* to be a forensic psychologist. I don't have a medical licence or deal with drugs, and I never will. Psychiatrists are doctors, psychologists do therapy. Plus, I still need a year of work experience to complete the qualification."

"Oh. So what do you actually do at the moment in the mental hospitals?" Dylan still looked confused.

She sighed. She'd explained it multiple times, but nobody seemed to understand her job at all. Even most of the hospital staff didn't understand it.

"I provide legal information about their rights and help support the patients in whatever they need. A psychiatric hospital is a scary place to be locked away in. Hell, it's a scary place to work in sometimes. And patients need support from an independent person who doesn't work for the hospital.

Especially if they're paranoid, which a lot are."

"But everyone you work with is some sort of mentally ill criminal?"

"No, Jesus, Dylan. Stereotype much? Well, I mean, yes, a lot *happen* to have a criminal record, but that doesn't mean they're dangerous, and it certainly isn't all of them." She rolled her eyes.

"What kind of criminal records?"

"Some are bad, some are not that bad." Her lips shut tight. They were getting way off subject here.

"Are we talking like serial killer bad?" The vein on his forehead was bulging the way it did when he was worried.

"I don't think so. Well, I mean, I don't always know what they've done. I couldn't say no for definite. I only know the crime if they tell me or if I look at their file, which I can only do with their permission. It's all a bit complicated, really."

"Oh. It sounds like a dangerous job, to be honest, Summer. Especially after that one who escaped the other month."

"It's really not dangerous. Not usually. I've only had a couple of patients turn on me unexpectedly. It's the nature of their illness, sometimes. And they escape all the time when out on leave. That wasn't unusual, either. They usually get caught pretty quickly. The truth is they are far more likely to be a victim of crime than a perpetrator."

"Do you ever deal with psychopaths?" He picked up the butter knife and waved it in a stabbing motion towards Summer. He really hadn't changed since they were teenagers.

"That's… more of a symptom, rather than a diagnosis. But yes, I work with people who display psychopathic tendencies sometimes. Now, can we talk about Eddie?" She desperately tried to get the conversation back to their brother.

Dylan whistled through his teeth. They fell silent as they spotted the waitress leaving the counter with two plates of toasties. Each sandwich was bursting with golden melted cheese, and the smell wafted over. Summer's stomach growled.

"Here you go, ducks. Enjoy." She plonked a plate in between each of them and walked off.

Summer saw a pink slice of ham sticking out from the edge of her toastie. "Here you go." She moved her plate in front of Dylan and took her sandwich from his side of the table. She picked up the toastie and took a large bite, enjoying the burst of flavour. Cheese had to be one of the best foods ever. Definitely in her top five. Dylan bit noisily into his own sandwich and swallowed it in half a second.

He still ate like a teenager, too.

"Still. I'm dead proud of you, sis. You've done amazing with all that school stuff. But I'd rather you worked somewhere safer. Especially after all that stuff with that other patient," he said, his vein popping again.

Summer didn't respond. She wasn't ready to admit to anyone that she sometimes thought the same. A patient had turned on her only the week before, thinking she was out to get him. It had been a simple conversation that went from friendly to dangerous in a split second when he suddenly accused her of wanting to murder him. Maybe she needed a new job. Especially with Joshua relying on her. He still had his dad, but her bond with Joshua was special. She couldn't stand the thought of him having to grow up without her.

Dylan was lost in his own thoughts as he tore through his toastie, looking down at the table. Summer ate hers more slowly, savouring each mouthful. She watched a lone mother and small child in the opposite corner of the cafe. They were eating their food together, the mother unable to sit and eat hers as she was too busy making sure the little girl had everything she needed. An ache for Joshua tugged at her heart. Her eyes were pulled to the clock above the family. Damn. It was time for her visit. She ate the last bite of her toastie and took a big gulp from the glass of coke.

"I'd better get on with some work," she said.

Dylan took the paper towel from the cutlery and wiped his mouth. At least he had *some* table manners.

"Where are you today?" he asked.

"A high security hospital."

After the conversation they'd just had about safety, there was no way she was going to admit which one. She didn't need to cause him any more worry.

"Well, be careful." He grabbed his black parka coat from the chair next to him and shoved his arms through the sleeves.

"Honestly, Dylan, it's as safe as houses." She smiled at him as she grabbed her own coat and handbag.

They left a few quid each on the table for the toasties and waved goodbye to the waitress as they left. The bell jingled once again as they walked out into the fresh air and the wind ran straight through Summer's open jacket, making her shiver.

"I'll pop by at the weekend after work, and we'll try to come up with some ideas for finding Eddie, OK?" Dylan wrapped his arms around her and squeezed.

"Yes, please." She squeezed him back.

Dylan released his grip and crossed the road to where he'd parked his work van. Summer turned around to walk home, before remembering she had driven and she'd parked her car right on the road behind her. She heard a laugh and saw Dylan grinning at her from across the road.

She stuck her middle finger up with a smile and jumped into her car, blowing on her freezing hands and cranking up the heat as soon as the engine was running. Try as she might, she couldn't shake a strange feeling she'd had since speaking to Dylan about her job. Had she jinxed herself?

Was her job too dangerous, considering she had Joshua?

She drove away with an unsettling dread that suggested Dylan might be right.

4

The Servant

I'd delivered the woman to Him as promised, but the peace I longed for hadn't come. Instead, I lay back on my bed, hands tight over my ears. I knew He was coming. He was coming for me and I deserved it. I'd done it wrong.

Again.

I shouldn't have touched her first.

I was too weak to resist once she was naked, and He'd known as soon as he saw her. I'd raced home to beg for forgiveness. Soon enough, a stench filled the room which infiltrated my nostrils so completely that it forced me to hold my breath to stop myself from gagging. And the familiar black shadow stared from its corner.

Dark pupils bored into my own. The pale hair on my scarred arms rose as goosebumps tickled my skin. My toes curled and my stomach ached from the knots deep inside. Every inch of my being warned me. *Danger*. I was in terrible danger.

My body didn't know whether to settle on fight or flight. I knew fighting the shadow was futile. But I knew flight wouldn't work either. The shadow would follow me anywhere.

So instead, the third, more cowardly option was the only one I managed. I froze.

I lay in my bed, hidden under the duvet cover. Naked. The soft blanket felt cool against my scarred skin. It was my only armour against the petrifying creature that was fixated on me. And I knew I must meet all demands. No matter what the cost, because the creature in front of me was not a creature at all, but a devil.

The devil.

And he was out for blood.

I knew what happened to those who defied Him. My lungs ached as breathing became more difficult. A rasping noise offended my ears so deeply it almost hurt. I felt my arms rise from under the blanket, as if someone else was controlling them, and shove a finger in each ear. But the rasp increased in volume. *Louder. Heavier. Deeper.*

Repeatedly, the noise cut into my eardrums. It was stuck inside my brain. I couldn't hear my thoughts as the rasp took over my mind until it was the only noise in existence.

"I see you." The rasping breath turned into a dark, gravelly voice. A whisper deep within my mind, but it wasn't my voice. No. It was the shadow. Though the shadow's thin lips never moved.

"Yes, Sir," I mumbled.

"You violated her," the voice said.

I nodded, knowing denial was futile. "I wanted to help, Sir. She needed to be more obedient."

"LIES! She was meant for me and you took her first."

I screamed and stuck my fingers deeper into my ears, though it was of no use against the voice in my head. "Sorry!" I shouted, "I will do better, Sir."

"I need you to *bring them* only. Choose someone you don't need to shape. You know what I need, bring them to me. I'll give you one more chance."

And with that, the shadow disappeared, and the room slowly brightened. Relief hit me, and I removed my fingers from my ears.

He was gone. Despite my misdemeanour, I had another chance. And this time I won't mess it up.

Because I knew exactly which woman to pick to make Him happy.

5

Swanson

An unusual sensation overcame Swanson as he weaved through the crowded main roads of Derby City Centre. His car was moving, as were the surrounding streets, yet he felt *still*. Lost in his own thoughts. He stopped at a red light and stretched one long leg to ease a creak in his knee. The glaring lights of a small roadside cash and carry caught his attention.

Fuck it.

He manoeuvred out of the stalled line of rush hour traffic and over to the pavement where the shop stood. He parked on the double yellow lines outside and ignored the glares from the other drivers. Let them look. Suspects glared at him every day.

He pushed open the heavy security door and marched inside the shop, heading straight to the counter. A spotty young man sat behind it on a tall, wooden chair. He dressed head to toe in a matching black tracksuit with two white lines running down the side of it. He barely looked old enough to sell the alcohol he sat in front of.

"Twenty of those and a lighter, please," he said to the boy, digging out his wallet and hoping he had some cash on him after noticing the 'no card machine' sign on the countertop. What kind of place didn't take card these days?

"Sure, mate." The boy barely looked up at Swanson before grabbing the cigarettes and tossing them over. "£9.59, please, mate."

Jesus. Last time he'd bought cigarettes they'd cost little more than a fiver. He tried to hide the shock on his face and threw a crumpled ten pound note on the counter. He marched back out of the shop without waiting for his change, his cigarettes and lighter in hand.

As soon as the frosty breeze hit his face, he pulled open the carton of cigarettes and dragged one out with his teeth. It had been five years since he'd last tasted the stale smoke of a cigarette, but his willpower was well and truly drained. What was the point in preventing cancer if he had a tumour already? Quitting nicotine clearly hadn't been worth the stress.

Although he certainly wasn't making it a daily thing at nearly a tenner a pop.

The first drag hit his throat hard as it swirled its way into his lungs. He blew it out immediately in one quick breath.

Urgh.

It did not taste as good as his memory allowed him to think it did. He sniffed deeply. It didn't even smell as good as he remembered.

Regardless, he took another drag and leant against the wall of the building next to the shop. The little buzz he got from each drag was worth it, for now. He scoped out his surroundings as he tried to get used to inhaling the smoke again. It took him a moment to realise where he was. He stepped forward, away from the wall, and looked around to double check. He was right.

Summer's flat was around the corner.

His feet moved before his brain connected with his body as an urge to be near Summer took over. He needed her calm. Her silly laugh. He rounded the corner and saw the cafe she liked was right across the road. *Barbara's Baps.* The cafe stuck out like a sore thumb on the residential street, an old, converted mid terrace house which someone had painted green and white. Though it had been a long time since a brush had been near it, judging from the chipped paintwork.

The windows were larger than the houses which surrounded it and as he glanced over, he instantly recognised Summer sitting near the left-hand window. A grin lined her lips, and she'd bunched her long brown hair to one side of her face so she could eat. She looked happy.

He hadn't often seen her happy. Between Lucy, Astrid, and Eddie, she hadn't had an easy couple of months. Her face lit up in a way he hadn't seen before.

Across from her, Swanson made out the back of a man's head, and he felt a heaviness in the pit of his stomach. The man clearly wasn't Aaron or Eddie. And yet he was the one who was making Summer so happy.

Good for her.

He stubbed out his cigarette and rounded the corner again to his car. Maybe work would be the best place to go after all. He needed a suitable case to get stuck into, and Hart clearly had something good to work on.

6

Summer

Summer felt the familiar anxiety in the pit of her stomach as she drove onto the winding dirt road that led to Adrenna Psychiatric Hospital. The hospital sat ten minutes outside of the city centre, the only one on her rota that she hated to visit. Though she hadn't pinpointed the reason why.

She put it down to knowing they wrongly incarcerated her brother there for so long. Being inside Adrenna was a secret glimpse into the lonely life he'd been living as a prisoner whilst she and Dylan lived freely.

That, and the fact Adrenna specialised in patients with personality disorders detained as criminals under a section 37/41. This included Narcissistic Personality Disorder, Antisocial Personality Disorder and Paranoid Personality Disorder, and essentially meant patients with a *violent* history inhabited it.

Her own brother had attempted to murder their mother in a fit of psychotic rage, but only after being tormented by what he thought to be a demon or devil for months. The only actual devil was his ex.

Surprisingly, no one had developed the land around Adrenna yet. So beautiful rolling fields still surrounded it. It would pose as the perfect, picturesque Sunday drive if looking at an image. But in person, it didn't have the usual peace of the countryside. Instead, the emptiness around the hospital contributed towards the unwelcome atmosphere.

The sun shone in Summer's eyes as she drove through the black iron gates of the hospital entrance. They had done little to update the decor since building Adrenna in the 1800s as an asylum for 'lunatics'. Few original asylums still stood in the UK, but Adrenna loomed tall as if proud of its dark history.

Maybe that was another reason for the creepiness.

From the old pictures Summer had seen online, it actually looked more foreboding now than when first built. It had been stunning at one time. The architect had clearly taken great pride in their work. But the gates no longer held their gothic prominence, welcoming visitors and patients alike. Weathering over the years had caused the iron to rust and become deformed, giving it a warped, crooked look. The red brick walls that surrounded either side of the gate were built twelve feet high originally, to keep the 'lunatics' inside. Though the walls still contained the hospital buildings, they now spalled from weather and lack of care, and the weaker parts crumbled with decay.

She sighed as her car crunched slowly over the gravelled car park to the right of the hospital. She'd jumped at the chance to cover Adrenna when her supervisor mentioned the previous advocate quit. Summer took it as a signal to keep looking for Eddie. Now he was missing it was the only way she'd be able to get to know him. There could be a clue here as to where Eddie was.

But that was before she'd found out the previous advocate quit due to stress from visiting Adrenna.

As with her previous four visits, Summer parked as far back from the grand building as possible. She needed no more patients finding out where she lived after Lucy.

She slung her old Radley handbag onto her shoulder and jumped out of the car, pulling the laptop bag from the boot before she headed to the entrance. The bracing wind was even stronger in the open space, and her hair whipped around her face. She pulled up the faux fur hood of her coat as far forward as possible. It might only be December, but bring on spring.

She took her time at first. The uneven gravel was tricky to walk on in her new, heeled boots, and she was in no rush to get inside. But a powerful gust flew straight into her hood, and she put her head down and quickened her pace to the front of the building.

The large entrance at the top of the stone steps was unimpressive compared to the rest of the building. Long ago, someone locked shut the old wooden doors with their peeling red paint, and nailed a wooden bar across them for good measure. The entrance had been unused for years. So she continued down the side of the building to a smaller door halfway down.

The dread grew in her stomach as she pulled down her hood to reveal her face and readied herself to press the intercom. She wondered if this was how Becky felt when pressing the intercom. If so, no wonder she quit.

A few seconds later, a loud buzzer rang out into the silence, followed by a clicking noise. She pushed open the door, entered the dark hallway and waited for the door to bang shut behind her. The bang of the door had almost given her a heart attack when she first visited, but she was used to it now.

THE HOSPITAL

The warm air in the hallway was stifling compared to the frostiness of the outside, and she wrangled her hand through the laptop bag strap to pull down the zipper of her coat. The grand staircase was adjacent to the doorway, but she ignored it and continued down the hall, her boots softened by the deep red carpet. As she reached the end of the corridor, she stopped, took a breath, and forced her face into a cheerful smile before opening the door.

The reception room was fairly small, but the bright white front desk immediately drew her eye to the left-hand side of the room. It was ugly and cheap, and far too modern compared to the other decor.

There were lockers on the right-hand side, and another corridor led around the back of the ugly desk. But the staff had never invited Summer down there. Which was unusual, as she should have access to the whole hospital as an advocate, but Summer didn't argue. The less she had to see of this place, the better.

"Morning," Summer said to the old bat behind the desk, which was encased in thick glass. The same receptionist was working every time she visited the hospital, yet she never revealed her name.

The woman looked up and smiled shortly. "Sign in here, please." She forced something A4 sized and hard through a gap in the glass window. It was the paper register and a black pen stuck to a wooden clipboard.

Summer took off her laptop bag and plonked it on the floor before she walked over and signed her name. She didn't bother saying another word to the woman, but awkwardly shoved the clipboard back through the hole, catching the corner on the top of the glass. The woman snatched it from her and threw her an angry look.

"Locker 16," she said, placing a ring of keys, an alarm, and a black belt through the hole.

Summer's face flushed, but she took the keys and belt with a 'thank you' and walked back to get her laptop bag. She removed her coat and placed it inside locker 16 with her handbag and laptop bag. The laptop wasn't allowed on the ward. Though it was a habit to bring it with her wherever she went in case she had to do research for a patient or write her notes before leaving.

She stole a glance at the old bat, who was looking down at her screen, and she snuck her phone into her pocket. Making sure it was well-hidden. She placed the belt that she'd given her around her waist with the ring of keys and alarm attached. The only other item she held was a notepad and pen, which she clutched close to her chest. She closed the locker door and left the room without a word, ignoring the sense of dread which built with every step.

7

Swanson

Swanson attempted to drive to the office, but found himself pulled over in the large supermarket car park nearby. The same place he'd first met Summer, right after a patient of hers kidnapped her. He remembered Hart struggling to calm the patient, and Summer swooping in calmly as anything to help. It was impressive. Most trained officers Swanson knew would have been far too traumatised to stay as calm as Summer had. Though it wasn't the most romantic of first encounters.

Maybe they were doomed from the start.

He wondered who the man was that made her laugh so much. She was clearly comfortable with him. He'd only spoken to her yesterday about finding her brother and she hadn't mentioned meeting anyone else. The police still officially wanted Eddie for questioning after Astrid had accused him of attempted murder. Though Astrid had also disappeared, which didn't bode well for her story's believability.

He got out of the car and leant against the cool metal as he lit another cigarette. His nose slowly turned numb in the cold air, and he rubbed his thumb against it absentmindedly as he smoked. People milled around him, mostly elderly people taking their time, or tired parents rushing around with a baby attached to them in one form or another. He should probably enter the shop and buy some mints to get rid of the cigarette breath. Hart would definitely smell it otherwise. He stepped forward to make a move to the entrance, but froze mid-step.

Two blank eyes stared straight at him. The eyes were clouded over with no visible pupil, but he felt their stare. They belonged to an old man, with a white beard and wispy hair, both running past his shoulders. His attire evidenced his need for a bath and a good meal.

But it wasn't the dirty appearance of the man which bothered Swanson.

Why was a blind man staring straight at him?

Swanson shifted his feet and turned away to pull once more on his cigarette, but when he glanced back, the man hadn't moved an inch.

He stubbed out the cigarette and climbed back into the car. He didn't have time for creepy old men today. Or the headspace to even think about it.

He grabbed his phone and flicked through the random notifications. He had a message from Hart asking where he was, and he sent her a quick reply to say he was getting breakfast. That should stall her, and a bacon wrap would make her moan less when he finally had the motivation to turn up.

He threw down his phone on the passenger seat and looked up with a sigh.

And his heart nearly jumped out of his chest.

The man with blank eyes was right outside his window, still staring straight at him.

8

Summer

Summer walked back down the corridor and up the staircase she'd ignored when first entering the dim building. The staircase appeared as if it should lead to a grand landing area with an opulent ballroom waiting for her. But instead it led to a claustrophobic landing area with three doors.

The doors were out of place and didn't quite fit in with the surroundings. They were modern oak, and strong. A pane of thick glass ran through the centre of each door as a safety measure. It allowed you to look into the room ahead before entering.

Each door led to a different ward. Ward A was the first door leading to the left-hand side of the building. Her plan was to head into Ward A first, as some patients there were trusting enough to chat to her. It was a ward for patients who were responding well to treatment and were no longer thought to be a risk to themselves or others. They were less paranoid and didn't suffer from psychotic delusions anymore, and therefore easier to make relationships with.

It was also the ward where Eddie spent the last year of his stay. His patient file might still be saved on the computer.

She walked over to the door of Ward A and peered through the glass. Although this ward was less risky, she still had to follow procedure and ensure there were no patients close to the door before she opened it. Most modern hospitals had air locked doors between wards and even on entry, so it was almost impossible for a patient to escape. But Adrenna only had one locked door to get off the ward, and one other locked door to the outside world. It wasn't much at all, really.

All she saw through the glass was an empty corridor. The coast was clear.

She pulled the keyring out of her belt and squinted at the peeling stickers on each one until she found the Ward A key. She double checked the coast was still clear, and opened up the door to a short corridor.

It was the opposite of the dark hallway downstairs, but far too cold to be homely. She strolled down the corridor and past the kitchen door, where a smell of burnt toast lingered. Patients living in Ward A were the only ones the staff trusted with their very own working kitchen, complete with a kettle and metal cutlery. Though they only allowed one patient in at a time. The room was small and difficult to supervise, and caution was still required. It wasn't always obvious if a patient suffered a relapse.

Past the kitchen, the corridor opened up into a spacious living area. This was also the only ward where the living area was a little more homely than the clinical corridor. They didn't encase the TV in a special protective case, they nailed it to the wall like people would in a lot of 'normal' homes. The sofas were all close together, and arranged in a U shape in front of the TV. There was an art room off to the right, where patients had access to art therapy on a Tuesday and Thursday, and they had a pool table in the far corner. Though the balls and cues were stored away in a locked unit, and only allowed out at certain times.

Another corridor led to the left and down to a locked gym. Patients had supervised daily access to the gym and to the computer room next door. The corridor to the right led to the bedrooms and isolation room; an empty room where patients stayed if they were trying to hurt themselves or others. There was a bed, a metal toilet, and a locked slip in the door for food. It was the last resort before forced medication.

Summer always stayed well away from that room. No patient in that room was in a safe enough frame of mind for her to talk to.

She scanned the ward and took in the current patients who were out of their rooms. A man Summer didn't recognise was walking away to the gym or computer room with a support worker. Bertie was sitting on the sofa. He was fairly new to Ward A, and his nervousness meant he didn't talk much, but she'd got the odd word out of him a few times.

Asif was sitting next to him, and Summer smiled when she saw him. He seemed to feel someone looking at him and raised his head to look around. His face lit up once he spotted her. Asif had taken to her straight away on her first official visit, and it was he who had given her a tour of the ward. Normally it would be the hospital manager or leading psychiatrist, but Summer was yet to meet the manager. She only knew her name was Glenda Kitching, and she was off sick. The leading psychiatrist, Dr Randall, was friendly, though. And had been far more welcoming than that receptionist downstairs.

"Hi, Summer!" Asif stood and rushed over to her as best as his limp would allow him to hurry.

Summer stepped forward to meet him. He was actually quite tall, but his bad leg caused a stoop that made him roughly the same height as her.

"Hi, Asif. How are you?"

"I'm OK. I could do with a chat. Is that OK?" Asif looked down as he spoke, a shy smile lined his lips.

"Of course we can. Where shall we chat?" She looked around the ward for a quiet space.

"Oh, here is fine. I have my ward round next week. Can you come in with me?" He spoke quickly, looked up, and wrung his hands together nervously.

The ward round was a regular multidisciplinary meeting where the different hospital specialists met with the patient to discuss their care.

She nodded. "Yes, I'd be happy too."

His face broke into another smile. "Oh, great, great. Thank you." He let out a short, much relieved giggle.

"You're welcome. Is there anything in particular you'd like me to do or say or do? Or do you want some moral support?" She imagined Asif being too shy to ask his doctor for something and needing her to ask for him, or maybe he wanted her to sit in whilst *he* asked for something.

He bowed his head, deep in thought. "I'll think about it," he decided.

That would be moral support, Summer mused. An idea came to her.

"OK. Am I allowed access to your file so I can prepare? No problem if you'd rather I don't. It's completely up to you."

"Oh yes, yes. That's fine." He nodded and gave her a big grin.

"Great." Summer gave him a moment to ask her for anything else, but he fell silent. His eyes flicked around the room. "Shall we sit on the sofa for a bit?"

He nodded, and they walked over together. A daytime talk show was playing on the TV. Bertie looked away from the show as they approached, and Summer asked him how he was doing. She made small talk with them both, counting down the minutes until she could reasonably disappear to look at the file. She waited about ten minutes to announce she had to do something and said goodbye to Asif and Bertie.

The nurses' station was a small room at the back of the open plan living area. It had a large window and was called the fish bowl by the patients. Nurses and ward staff could do paperwork there whilst still monitoring the patients in the living area. It was where the computer was, and all paper patient files, too.

As Summer walked over, she made a mental note of where the staff were on the ward. She saw a couple of nurses in the medication room, which had a door like a horse stable where only the top half opened. Ward A didn't have as many staff members as other wards, as no patients required two-to-one care or 24-hour supervision, and there were no other support workers around the living area.

She pulled out the ring of keys from the belt bag and selected the small black key with a sticker that said 'stations'. It was a strange, circular shape, and the same key opened each of the stations on each ward. Unlike the ward doors which had a different key for each. She glanced through the large window and made sure it was empty before letting herself in.

The room was small and stuffy. Cupboards lined the far wall from floor to ceiling. Summer knew that was where they kept the paper files for the patients, but she hadn't found Eddie's when she looked the other week. She wasn't actually sure what happened to the files once the patient transferred to a different unit. Maybe they followed the patient. That would make sense. They had sent Eddie to a different, low security unit right before he disappeared completely. It was like a halfway house, and easy for him to run away from once Astrid accused him of attempted murder.

In the corner nearest to Summer sat a computer with electronic files on each patient. And now, thanks to Asif, Summer had the perfect excuse to log in and review the files.

She checked her notepad for the password they had provided her with during her first visit to the hospital and logged in to the hospital's guest account. Her fingers drummed against the desk, and she glanced up periodically to look through the window.

She opened Asif's file first and briefly flicked through. His doctor diagnosed him with Narcissistic Personality Disorder and the court had convicted him for stalking an ex-girlfriend for six months, eventually attacking her in her own home. *Christ.* He was so sweet Summer couldn't imagine him acting like that.

She left his file open on one tab and used a secondary tab to flick through the names of each patient file looking for Eddie. There was nothing, but she fought away the disappointment. She wasn't giving up that easily.

She used the search bar on the file screen instead and typed in 'Eddie Thomas'. Hope gripped her as a folder in his name finally popped up. She double clicked on the folder with his name, and different files appeared in a list before her.

'Ward Round Record'

'Medication Sheet'
'Patient History'

She hesitated. These were highly private and personal to Eddie. It felt so wrong to even be this close to reading them. Would he be OK with her opening them up?

She thought about him being alone somewhere on a dark street in the freezing wind. He would be alone at Christmas in a few weeks. An ache tugged at her heart, and she opened the most recent file, which was a ward round record. It was the meeting minutes from his final ward round at Adrenna Hospital.

Summer skim read through the report with a smile. The discussion had centred around how well Eddie was doing, and how happy he was to be transferring to a low secure unit.

But a noise at the door made her heart thump. She quickly closed the file and brought up Asif's instead. She looked up, smiling at the nurse who entered the station and praying she didn't look as guilty as she felt.

"Hello." The young nurse smiled at her.

"Hi," Summer said with a big smile that she was sure made her look guilty of something. "I'm just checking a patient file. Do you need the computer?"

"Oh, no problem. It can wait," she replied, waving a hand away.

"No, no. Here you go." Summer logged off and stood up from the computer chair. "I'm finished, anyway."

The nurse gave her a cautious smile before taking the computer chair. The staff were always on best behaviour around an advocate like Summer.

She locked the nurse in the fishbowl room and threw a glance at her watch. She really needed to move on to the other wards.

Ward B wasn't so bad. Their patients were midway and often super quiet. So it made sense to get Ward C out of the way. That was the most precarious ward.

The patients of Ward C were new and not yet responding to medication or therapy. They could be violent and difficult to manage. As an advocate, Summer didn't receive any kind of training in restraint or protecting herself. Despite many requests to her supervisor to be trained in defending herself safely, and Adrenna being home to some of the country's most dangerous patients, her concerns fell on deaf ears.

It wasn't the patients that bothered Summer, though. It was the staff. They were mostly young people who thought working at Adrenna would be cool. Or someone had told them it would be rewarding. But in reality, they were poorly trained, overworked, and disillusioned. Being on Ward C made her anxiety skyrocket because she had no faith in the staff to keep her safe if a patient had a psychotic episode or other violent outburst. She got the feeling that they would be more likely to run away and save themselves. And she didn't blame them.

She took a moment to steel herself outside Ward C's door and peered through the glass section. There was no corridor in Ward C, and instead it opened out straight into the living area. She saw a few patients and staff, and the sense of foreboding made her feel sick. She unlocked the door anyway and closed it quickly behind her.

The ward was fairly quiet. Doctor Randall, the only senior member of the team that she had spoken to so far, had explained to her previously that these patients were on heavier medications, and they were often drowsier than the other wards as a result.

There was one patient wandering around with a vacant look,

as if lost in his own world. Summer watched him for a moment. She'd love to know where he'd taken himself in his own mind. Hopefully, somewhere nicer than here.

There was another person in particular she had hoped to see, though. There were a couple of nurses on the ward and she walked over to an older lady she recognised, Beth. She'd been nice to Summer the previous week and actually struck up a conversation. She stood in the corner with a clipboard in her hand, looking down at it intensely.

"Hi," Summer smiled at her.

Beth looked up and gave Summer a warm smile. "Hey, Summer isn't it?"

Summer nodded. "I wondered if Aaron was around today?" she asked as casually as she could.

"Oh no, he hates earlies. He doesn't enjoy getting out of bed, the lazy sod." The nurse laughed.

Summer joined in with the laughter to hide her disappointment. She hadn't known Aaron hated earlies, though it occurred to her Aaron had mostly done the late shift at Derby Psychiatric Hospital.

"OK, I'll sit down for a bit and see if anyone wants to chat," Summer replied.

She strolled over to the sofas in the middle of the room and took a seat close to a patient named Andy, who sat in grey jogging bottoms and a matching jumper. He was looking at the floor, unblinking. Summer said nothing to him. He'd been the same last week and didn't appear to be a threat. She chose the middle of the room so patients could easily see her there if they wanted her help, and staff could easily see her should she need their help.

Yet a sudden chill reached her, and the hairs on the back of her neck stood up. She shifted uncomfortably in her seat and looked around. Two dark eyes were staring straight at her from around the ward corner. They disappeared before she had time to see the person's face.

"Who's that?" she muttered out loud.

"The Devil. You mustn't go near the Devil." Andy said.

Summer nearly doubled over in shock at hearing him speak. She turned back to him. He still stared at the floor.

"What was that, Andy? Are you OK?"

His head snapped up, his dark, narrow eyes stared into Summers. Her hand went to her alarm.

"The Devil is coming for you."

9

The Servant

The corridor to the dining area loomed before me. It was a pathway full of danger. People getting too close as they passed, or hiding behind doors. Corridors were plain dangerous. But I told nobody in Adrenna about that.

That was crazy talk, apparently.

I turned to face the quiet room behind me instead, but I still heard the low rasping of the shadow that laid within. I couldn't go back inside there unless I had what he requested.

I chose the wrong woman. I'd had to violate her to make her more humble, and I was not allowed to do that. But He had forgiven me. Well, He *would* forgive me. As long as I get it right the next time.

And I wouldn't sleep until I had.

So I was stuck on the threshold of the door. I had to choose between the wrath in my room or the unknown horrors of the corridor. A laugh trickled down the corridor. A soft, sweet laugh. One I knew.

The one the Devil wanted.

The corridor spun before me and seemed to get longer with each passing second. I kept my weapon in my hand and squeezed my fingers around it, not caring that it might cut my fingers.

I crept down the corridor, but stumbled and grabbed a hold of the wall. I took a deep breath and allowed the dizziness to pass.

I cursed myself and rubbed away the twitch in my eye. I needed to man up and make it to her. This was a risk for me. I had never killed before. But it was her or me.

And I would always choose myself.

The corridor righted, and I continued down the white tiles. My nerves were on edge, but nothing jumped out from behind any doors this time. I reached the end safely and peered around the corner to the living room of the hospital. A large room with huge, locked windows and sofas lining the edge of the walls, and dotted about the middle of the room.

There was an armchair in the middle of the room, near the TV, and there she was. Her long hair hung past her breasts. Her pretty face smiled at one of the other patients. The patient wasn't responding. Few of them did. They were fed too many drugs.

But that suited me fine.

I looked over to the far corner of the room to the nurses' station, a small room surrounded by thick glass. Two nurses were inside and chatting with each other. They smiled and laughed as if telling jokes to each other. They were probably joking about patients. I heard them joking inappropriately all the time. But I didn't care. I was glad they were distracted.

I surveyed the rest of the ward. One patient sat in the corner in an armchair. He wore the hospital's own grey tracksuit bottoms and matching jumper. Patients didn't have to wear them, but they were comfortable and handy for people who didn't have many clothes. Which apparently was most patients, in this ward at least. The most dangerous patients were on this ward supposedly, but actually they were so drugged up it was difficult for them to be dangerous to anyone. He stared at the floor. I watched him for a moment. He didn't blink once.

Another patient in the tracksuit walked around in circles on the left side of the room. He moaned to himself quietly and clasped his hands together. He was smiling, and clearly happy in his own world.

Two nursing assistants busied themselves with the last patient, trying to get him to stand so he could go for his nap. I made it a point not to learn their names.

They wouldn't be around long enough for it to matter.

I peered at the woman. I forgot her full name, but her first name was Summer. Beautiful. If you ever thought about what the season of Summer looks like as a person, it would be her. It was her name that drew the devil to her at first. And her voice. Her soft, quiet voice. She walked as though she was afraid of nothing, but I saw fear in her eyes. It had interested me, and the devil saw her through me.

She was our new advocate. I'd tried to get the last one for the Devil, but it hadn't gone to plan. I'd only wanted to talk to her, but the Devil wanted more. Needed more.

When the patient did not respond, Summer looked around the room. She turned and spotted me, and I saw her eyes squint at me. My head snapped back around the corner, and I stood still for a moment. A few seconds passed, and I dared to look again. She wasn't looking, but the patient was talking to her, and he looked intense.

I stalked over to the middle of the ward, confident in my stride. My thoughts only focused on her because if I thought too much, I'd lose my nerve. I walked straight up to the pretty girl with the sing-song laugh who looked like Summer.

I unleashed the hidden razor blade from my fist.

And I gave her to the Devil.

10

Swanson

Swanson paused for a moment, his eyes closed tight, and allowed one last bitter breeze to wash over beads of sweat gathered on his forehead. His jaw clenched, he yanked open the entrance to the Derbyshire Police Station.

It opened straight into a bright room with a long desk lining the left-hand side. The powers that be, who were in charge of the wallet, recently gave the building funding to update the station decor. The sour smell of fresh paint still lingered. It wasn't a smell he could handle well. He took a deep breath and held it in his chest to keep the nausea at bay.

There were a couple of people keeping the two receptionists busy, so he kept his head down and walked straight through to the security door at the back, using his ID card to open the digitalised lock. Once safely in the corridor, he stood still and let out his breath in one big whoosh. He closed his eyes briefly to gather himself before he walked to the end of the corridor. There, the smell of paint lessened, replaced with the smell of cheap coffee from the nearby kitchen. Which wasn't too much better for Swanson's nausea.

Over the past few weeks, Swanson had sneakily commandeered a cupboard sized office to the left of the corridor. It was more of a storage area these days, but it was useful for the peace it provided him away from the primary set of open offices. They had designed the spaces to encourage 'working together' apparently. But they were noisy and off-putting. Ridiculous, really.

His anxiety lessened as he looked forward to sitting in silence at his desk and having some time to process the shit show that was his hospital appointment. But he opened the door to DI Hart perching on the edge of his makeshift desk. Her legs crossed. *Fuck sake.*

An open paper file was in her hands and she peered down at it. Her dark bob had fallen forward, partially blocking her face. But she looked up as he entered and shook her hair back. She didn't smile at him. Instead, her mouth set in a determined grimace.

"We've got a right one, here," she said.

"Hello to you, too," Swanson replied, still standing in the doorway. He thought about walking away, but didn't have the energy. She'd only run after him, anyway.

"Yes, yes. Hello." She waved her hand impatiently, snapped the file shut, and held it out for him.

Swanson sighed. "What now?" He ambled over to his desk and took the file from her. It was light. There wasn't much intel yet.

He squeezed past Hart, who made no attempt to move out of his way, and sat down at the desk. He opened it up and forced himself to focus, taking his time with the content. Hart would know something serious was wrong if he made even the tiniest of uncharacteristic movements. The first page in the file revealed a white-tiled floor, pristine apart from the large amount of deep red blood in the middle.

"Jeesh," Swanson said.

It reminded him of a recent incident with a young boy and his mother - the missing Astrid. He pushed the memory away and tried again to focus.

"Is that a hospital floor?" he asked.

Hart stood up and stepped away from the desk, turning in one smooth motion to face him. She folded her arms and nodded solemnly.

"What happened?" he asked.

"Do you know that big old hospital in the middle of nowhere? I think it's called Adrenna."

"I think so."

Swanson knew the hospital. He'd given the address to Summer to help her sneak in and look for her brother.

"Well, a member of staff was attacked a couple of hours ago by a patient. He was suffering from psychosis associated with paranoid schizophrenia. He sliced her neck and cut the hand of a doctor in the process. We need to have a chat with the doctor, and with the patient when possible."

"Why us? Is she pressing charges?" Swanson asked.

"Are you not awake yet? They have sliced her in the neck, Swanson. We might be looking at murder." She sighed and looked at him as if he was an idiot.

"Oh, yes, sorry. I didn't hear you properly. When was the last update?" He tried to keep his face normal, but what the hell expression did he normally pull anyway? It's not like he took note of his own facial expressions.

She uncrossed her arms and cocked her head, eyeing him warily. "A few minutes ago. She's still in surgery. Are you sure you're OK? I thought you were bringing breakfast like two hours ago?"

"Wouldn't be here if I wasn't. And yeah, I got distracted. I saw Summer and some weird old man nearly gave me a heart attack."

"What? Summer was with a weird old man?"

"No! I saw her for a moment in a cafe, and then an old man was being weird with me in the car park of the supermarket. He came right up to my car and stared. Nearly gave me a heart attack."

Hart erupted in a sudden belly laugh. He raised an eyebrow at her.

"Sorry, it's too funny thinking of you fearing an old man. What did he do?"

"Nothing. He didn't say a word, so I drove off."

"He was probably on drugs. I've seen you tackle worse things than a staring old man, Swanson! Have you lost your touch?" She laughed again before wiping a tear from one eye. "Have you asked Summer out yet?"

"Why would I do that?" he responded a little too quickly.

"Oh, OK. Sure. You be all surly and pretend you don't like her." She rolled her eyes. "You might smile more if you had a date lined up, and that would save *me* looking at your miserable face all the time. What did the old man look like if he scared you that much?"

"Some homeless guy with white eyes. It was weird. End of story." He waved his hand and sat up in the chair.

He'd driven away from the old man without checking if he was OK. Instead, he'd driven straight to a disused car park and slept for an hour.

"So are we going to this Adrenna place or what?" he asked.

"Alright, come on. You say that like I've *not* been waiting for you all morning." She turned and stalked out of the office, closing the door behind her.

Swanson stood a little too quickly. His vision blurred, and the room turned upside down. He closed his eyes, waiting for it to pass. After a moment, the dizziness stopped. He needed to eat something. He followed Hart into the corridor, but she'd disappeared.

He walked back through to the reception with his head down once again, and into the car park where he'd parked his Audi. He knew there was a Mars bar in the glove compartment. Just what he needed to get his blood sugar up.

Hart stood on the steps outside the entrance waiting for him. Her car keys swung in hand.

"I'm driving," she said, a determination set on her face.

Swanson scoffed. Hart rarely drove because he hated her erratic driving. He didn't know if he could put up with her lead right foot and angry braking today of all days.

"What? Why would I let you drive me?" he said.

"Because whether or not you want to admit it, you're ill." Her face softened.

Swanson immediately stood taller, his jaw set tight. "What do you mean I'm *ill*?"

"Don't insult me! I know you too well, and I can tell by looking at you that you're not well. You need to be at home, but you won't go, no matter what I say. So I'll allow you to stick with me on this one, but I'm driving, and you're going to tell me what's wrong."

She jiggled her car keys in front of him and turned to the red Astra to her left, which lit up as she pressed the key fob.

Swanson huffed. "I'm fine."

He wanted to argue, but a lack of energy made him follow Hart to her car. Despite his mammoth morning nap in the car, he'd woken up feeling worse. They got in the car and buckled up, and Hart swung them around in one effortless movement to pull out of the car park.

"So, what did the doctor say?" she asked as soon as they were on the main road which led to the city. They'd have to go through the centre to get to Adrenna, which was way out on the other side of the city in the quiet countryside

Swanson held his silence. *What was he supposed to say? He had a brain tumour? He needed a biopsy? What would she say and how would she react?*

He didn't want her sympathy; he wanted normality. "I don't really want to talk about it."

"Oh. It was that bad, eh? Hmm. We'll do this visit to Adrenna, then we'll go to yours and chat." She nodded as if agreeing with herself.

Swanson laughed at her unwarranted confidence. Though if anyone else gave him such orders, he wouldn't have had the same reaction.

"I said I don't want to talk about it."

"Oh, sorry. Didn't I mention that's not an option? You tell me or… I'm telling your Aunt Barb there's something seriously wrong and you won't tell anyone." Hart grinned at her own threat and glanced over at him.

"OK, OK. You win." Swanson leaned back in the car seat and rested his aching head.

He was enjoying being driven round for once, not that he'd ever admit it. He shifted in his seat. His whole body ached rather than just his head. So much for the painkillers working. It was strange having a tumour. Maybe he was aching from napping in a car, or maybe it was another symptom of his illness. How did people know? Worrying about it took more of a toll than the actual symptoms did.

His eyes were heavy with the gentle sway of the car. It felt good to close them for a moment as his head rocked against the headrest. Hart always cranked her heating way too high, but for once the warm air felt good. Cosy. The skies opened, and he listened to the gentle pitter patter of the rain on the roof of the car.

But a quick shake from Hart rudely awoke him.

"Sorry, but we're here," she said, peering at him with her head cocked to one side. "Either my driving has improved tenfold, or you're seriously ill. Which one are you willing to admit to?"

Swanson rushed to sit up. A deep heat filled his cheeks, and he turned away from her to look out of the window.

"I'm fine," he said, but the world spun again as the blood rushed to his head, and he closed his eyes until it stopped.

"Clearly you're not, though. Tell me what's wrong. You're worrying me now. Do you need some water?"

He heard her fumbling about, presumably looking for water. The dizziness passed, and he laughed.

"No! I don't want your mouldy old half-drunk water bottle. I sat up too quickly, is all. I haven't eaten. We can talk about my issues *after* we're finished here like we agreed. Come on." He unbuckled his seatbelt and gripped the door handle.

Hart didn't move.

"If you don't tell me now, I'm going to go into that hospital worrying about it rather than thinking about the case. I won't do my best job, and neither will you because you're totally off your game already, no offence. We'll miss seriously important details and the guy might get away with it and the woman might die with no justice and it will be all your fault Alex Swanson, so stop being macho and spit it—"

"I have a brain tumour," Swanson interrupted.

One thing he hadn't considered about being ill was the guilt he would feel at having to tell other people and watch *them* get upset. As soon as the words were out, he knew he'd done the wrong thing. As he watched Hart's shocked face a guilt settled within him, one that was going to stay for a while.

11

The Servant

I lay in my bed facing the ceiling. The rasping breath of the Devil was silent again. The bright bedroom light burned my eyes, even though they were closed. I made no move to turn it off. I liked the warmth of it bearing down on me.

The Devil always brought the dark with him.

Though I was grateful the Devil thought me good enough to assist him, I needed some sleep. I couldn't deny a slip of happiness at being able to sleep in peace for the first night in weeks. That's what He had promised me in exchange for doing his bidding.

As my mind quietened, I drifted off into another world. My favourite world. I was a small child again. Dad was sitting by the fire and telling me stories of grandad. Grandad cleansed the world, and Dad did too. Like I would grow to do the same thing. I would become a doctor, and work with those who saw things other people didn't.

Crazy people.

That's what the closed minded of the world called them. Some of them were ill and seeing things that weren't there, but sometimes Dad would find someone special. Someone special enough to be given to the Devil.

The Devil also liked women. He wanted the perfect woman and was on a constant search. Dad said Grandad had failed the Devil, but he wouldn't make the same mistake. He would find the perfect woman, and a protector for her so she wasn't a drain on the Devil.

But Dad did fail Him, like I almost had. Summer was the perfect woman, and now I needed to find her a protector.

12

Swanson

Hart froze mid-sentence, her mouth still open. She said nothing for a moment and simply stared at him. Their eyes met in the awkward silence. Swanson racked his brain for something clever to say. A joke. A noise. Anything.

They were never awkward with each other. The damn tumour was ruining things already. She shifted in her seat and looked away out of the windscreen.

"Oh. Well, that sucks," she said, her mouth finally closing.

Swanson didn't take his eyes off her. He wasn't sure what reaction he had expected, but not that.

"Is that all you have to say?"

She turned to face him again and shrugged. Her mouth opened, then closed as she found no words. A slow grin spread across Swanson's face.

"That sucks?" he repeated.

A deep need to laugh at her blank face built up. He held his breath and clamped his lips shut to keep the laughter at bay. The effort made his face turn a pale shade of red. But it was no use. As soon as he took a breath, he couldn't prevent the elongated snort of laughter that led to a deep, belly laugh when he saw Hart's eyes open wide. Though it only took a split second for her own shock to turn to a grin, and within seconds, they were both wiping away tears.

It took a few minutes for their laughter to fade away and silence to return. He felt Hart staring again and glanced over at her. She was giving him a strange look. Despite knowing her so well, it wasn't an expression he recognised. She spent most of her time either locked into a hard set grimace or laughing. Hart was not an in-between kind of person with emotions.

"You'll be fine, you know. It will take more than some stupid tumour to kick your fat arse," her face returned to its normal stoical glower and she looked away as she unbuckled her seat belt.

He nodded, though he knew she was full of rubbish. He still felt calmer as he reached for his own seatbelt and got out of the car.

The heavy pressure that had sat in his gut all morning eased somewhat at having admitted his problem to Hart. The light pitter patter of the rain felt cool against his cheeks, which also helped. Rain was the best weather. Memories of wet walks through the Peak District and Kinder Scout climbs danced in his mind. Maybe that's what he needed to do this week. Get out again and focus on walking. It was always better in the rain. The tourist walkers, mainly from London, disappeared. Leaving only the odd passerby to nod to as he hiked through the vastness of the Peak District hills, feeling unimportant in comparison. Lost. Peaceful.

And it wasn't often Swanson felt small. He'd always stuck out like a sore thumb in any room. Admittedly, the impressive

Victorian building towering in front of him made him feel almost miniscule.

Hart had parked in the depressing gravel car park to the right of the building, and he was glad he hadn't brought his own car here after all. It would be far too easy to get a chip from a flying piece of gravel, and that stress was the last thing he needed.

"Jesus, look at that van." Hart pointed to a van in the corner of the car park. It was an old campervan which the owner had not kept well maintained. The large, rear windows were painted black, or black with mud. It was hard to tell.

Swanson scanned the area, but other than the hospital, all he saw were the tall grey walls which encased the hospital grounds. It was a shame the walls were so high. Surely the beautiful views of rolling hills would be far more calming for patients than brick walls.

Though Adrenna Hospital did not appear to be a peaceful place to rest and get better. There was a fierceness to the aura of the building that was distinctly unwelcoming. Swanson couldn't put his finger on what it was exactly, but abrasive came close to describing it. Or unnerving.

The building was shaped like a square U, with colossal stone turrets at each angle. Despite the grim atmosphere, it was a fantastic example of early Victorian architecture using once beautiful white limestone, though it had grown grey over years of weathering. He whistled through his teeth.

"It's bloody scary as hell. I dunno what you're whistling at," Hart said as she walked towards the hospital, her feet crunching over the gravel. "Can you imagine being forced to live here? I think I'd stab someone, too. I'd prefer prison."

"Well, no. That's actually a good point." He didn't disagree with her for once. As impressive as the building was, the atmosphere that surrounded it was suffocating. It was as if the ancient building had formed its own personality over the decades.

And it wasn't a nice one.

"Imagine the stories those walls would tell if they spoke. All those old stories you hear about how mentally ill people used to be treated," she threw him a grim look, "shackles and lobotomies and that."

"Well, hopefully it can tell us a thing or two about this poor nurse who was stabbed."

"Yep. Come on." Hart hurried to the front of the building with her head down against the rain. Unlike Swanson, she hated the rain and would do anything to avoid getting stuck in it.

Swanson followed at a much slower pace. A part of him hoped something would call him away, so he didn't have to go inside. But his long strides meant he arrived at the entrance at exactly the same time as Hart, whose head only reached his shoulder on a good day, depending on her choice of shoe. In front of them grey stone steps led to grand double doors, with no discernible handle or doorbell.

"What the hell? How do you suppose we get inside?" Hart looked up at him with a tilted head.

"Let's look around the side." Swanson strode over to the right-hand turret and continued around the corner. Hart hurried after him.

A deep scream echoed all around them and stopped them dead in their tracks. It vibrated off the high walls that surrounded them. They glanced at each other, and began to run.

13

The Servant

I was waiting next to the window when a red car pulled up in the car park. It wasn't a car I'd seen before, and it set my nerves alight. The driver parked quickly, but didn't get out. It was like they wanted to keep me waiting.

They wanted me to suffer.

I craned my neck to see who was inside, but the driver wasn't visible. I saw someone's legs in the passenger seat. So there were two of them. I guessed they were talking.

Were they talking about me?

I waited with bated breath to see what they did. It felt like aeons had passed by the time they left the car. I took a step back from the window, but observed them carefully.

A woman with what I can only describe as a hard face stepped out of the driver's side. She wore a fitted grey suit and her dark hair in a short bob. That wouldn't do for the devil. He liked more feminine women and longer hair. She stumbled as she walked across the gravel in heels to meet the passenger who had also exited the car. She had the grace of a caffeinated ape.

The passenger was a man, also wearing a suit. He hunched his broad shoulders as he walked and his eyes flickered everywhere checking out his surroundings. He was obviously the type who was always on high alert. Despite his size, he was far more graceful than the tiny woman. I recognised him instantly.

My escape from the devil had arrived.

I continued to watch as they approached the stone steps at the front of the building and stared up at the inaccessible front door with confused faces. So, they hadn't visited before, and they were wearing suits.

Police.

I backed further away from the window. I needed a distraction.

I glimpsed at the living area behind me. It was not quite lunchtime and most patients were still in bed. Bobby was quite close to me. He was on his own, walking in circles as usual and humming to himself. He was off his bloody rocker and had the mind of a child.

Well, a child who did terrible things. Though he'd known no other way after his own upbringing.

Bobby wouldn't notice a thing. Destined to be forever trapped in his own little world. But there were also two nurses in the living area. One was sitting on the sofa, trying to coax a small patient named Baz out of his pyjamas. Baz was ignoring her and turning away. The other was distracted by the narcissistic prick, Samuel. He was demanding his medication early. Samuel was a first class arsehole. The man was not ill. He was lying to get an easy time of it after murdering his wife. He said the Devil made him do it, but I knew that was a lie because I asked the Devil myself.

THE HOSPITAL

I noted Samuel was about to walk away, and he would walk right past Bobby.

My hand clasped around the razor blade in my pocket, and I timed my route. I turned towards the window and slashed my arm. Nothing too bad, a small gash, and then I stalked over to Bobby just as Samuel was passing.

What happened next was a blur. I pushed Bobby into Samuel and sliced Bobby at the same time. All three of us fell into a heap on the floor. Bobby screamed like a wild animal, followed by a roar from Samuel.

The nurses sounded an alarm and ran towards us. More of them appeared within seconds as the alarm rang out through the hospital and other staff appeared. One slipped on the pool of blood leaking from either Bobby or Samuel. The scene was fast becoming a blur, and I wasn't entirely sure which one I'd stabbed.

My legs shook violently as I stood and moved away and pointed at Bobby and Samuel so the nurses would run to them first and stay away from me. I'd sort my wound alone.

Bobby sobbed. I noted one nurse took off his jacket to inspect his wound, so it must have been him I stabbed. Good. That was the plan. Samuel shouted at Bobby for knocking him over, not daring to say anything to me.

More staff came tunnelling into the ward to help, and surrounded Bobby and Samuel. I looked out the window and no longer saw the detectives, but they wouldn't be allowed on the ward whilst a serious incident was occurring.

I relaxed.

There would be no police interrogation today.

But I needed to see that man again. The Devil needed him, and it was my job to bring Him what he wanted.

14

Swanson

Swanson's loafers thudded off broken concrete slabs as he sprinted down the side of the building, looking for a way inside Adrenna. He heard Hart panting behind him, hot on his heels.

The screaming stopped, but it was blood curdling enough to know somebody was badly hurt. Halfway down the building a steel security door jutted out from the grey brick. It was so out of place against the Victorian backdrop it threw Swanson for a moment.

He almost skidded on the escaped gravel as he reached the door. He pulled the handle, but it was locked and didn't budge at all.

"There," Hart pointed to the wall next to the door. Her breath came in short, sharp pants.

Swanson followed her finger and spotted a wonky intercom screwed on to the wall. He reached out and pressed the button. A buzzing noise blared out through the silence, but nobody answered. He waited a moment, then pressed again, but held his finger down for longer.

"Yes?" a crackly, female voice said through the intercom, obviously unimpressed with the interruption.

"Er... hello." Swanson threw a look at Hart. She waved at him to continue on. "Can you let us in? We can hear someone in distress."

There was a moment of silence before the voice replied.

"And you are?"

"Detective Inspector Alex Swanson, and this is my colleague, Detective Inspector Rebecca Hart. Is everything OK? We heard a scream?"

He heard a quick snort from the mystery woman, that sounded suspiciously like laughter. Swanson stole another glance at Hart. She stared at the intercom, looking as confused as he felt.

"That was one of the patients acting up, I'm afraid. It's nothing to worry about. Not for you, anyway," the snotty woman responded.

"We're here about the earlier stabbing, actually, and just heard the scream a few moments ago. It really sounded like someone was hurt." Hart answered this time. Her forehead creased in a way which suggested she was about to lose her temper at any second. "Now please let us in so we can assess for ourselves what we need to worry about."

"Oh, of course you can come in to discuss the earlier stabbing." The woman sounded ultra polite suddenly. "I meant that the *recent* scream you heard is nothing to worry about. Nobody was hurt. Not physically, it was a distressed patient, and it is being dealt with."

"It?" Hart mouthed at him.

He shrugged in response. This place was worse than he thought. A buzzing noise came from the steel door, which was followed by a click to signal the lock opening. Swanson swiftly pulled it open and stepped inside. Hart followed so closely behind him she stood on the back of his loafer.

"Sorry, my bad" she mumbled and stepped next to him instead.

They stood inside the door, both hesitant to move any further into the building. Swanson had been in a few psychiatric hospitals as a part of his role and expected to enter some sort of busy reception area. But Adrenna was unlike any of the other hospitals he had visited.

The hallway was empty and silent. And if he'd thought the building was unwelcoming from the outside, the inside was far worse. The creep factor was exacerbated by dark red walls encasing the long corridor laid out ahead of them. To the left of the corridor was a staircase. There were no signs anywhere to show where the reception might be, though at the end of a corridor lay another door.

"Which way do you think? Stairs or door?" Hart's voice was much smaller than usual, which was strange considering she couldn't even whisper quietly.

Swanson shrugged. He strained his ears for any further screams, or any other noise, but heard nothing. His eyes searched the dark walls once more, yet there was no hint or direction signs anywhere.

"Let's try the door first. It seems the most likely place for a reception," he said.

Christ, if someone had been hurt they would never get there in time to help at this rate. He should've asked Summer to come. She'd been here at least once before; she might have been useful. Especially with patients. Maybe even the staff. He supposed they'd be nicer to her with her visiting regularly.

They stepped away from the door and it slammed shut behind them with a loud clunk. He saw Hart's hand fly up to her chest, but said nothing. He'd reserve the piss taking for when she was no longer freaked out.

And when his own heart had stopped pumping a million miles an hour.

"Must be one of those safety self-closing mechanisms," Swanson said to himself more than anything. Having a heart attack on top of a brain tumour surely wouldn't be a good mix.

"If you say so. You first. It's bloody creepy in here." Hart pointed to the door at the end of the corridor.

Swanson stepped in front of her and treaded softly up the corridor, his feet quiet against the carpet. She followed behind him, close enough that he heard her slow breathing. The warm air clung to him from all angles and felt suffocating. Beads of sweat formed on his forehead. Fuck staying inside here too long. He already couldn't wait to get outside again.

A feeling of reluctance swept over him as he reached the door. Christ, what was wrong with him? He cleared his throat and threw the door open before swallowing a sigh of relief as it opened up into a reception room. A large and ugly front desk to the left gripped his attention immediately. It was bright white and a stark contrast to the older, much darker surroundings.

A grey-haired woman sat behind it sporting thick glass and an oversized, pale blue cardigan. She wore her hair in a tight bun and crossed her plump arms against her substantial chest. The woman eyeballed him through her large, oval specs with one eyebrow raised and no smile.

Swanson gave what he hoped was a warm smile regardless, praying she would lighten up if he showed her he meant no harm or drama. He may as well attempt to be friendly. Hart followed in behind, and the old bag looked her up and down, making no attempt to hide her disapproval. Swanson moved forward a few steps.

"Good morning," he said.

"Morning," she replied, her face still set in the same sullen grimace. "How can I help?"

"We're here to talk to a Dr James Randall?" Hart piped up. She returned the woman's surly tone.

Swanson cleared his throat and covered his mouth as he did so to hide his grin. Rude old people were one of Hart's many pet hates. And he knew she was going to whine about this woman for days.

"What about, please?" The old bag asked.

"We're not at liberty to disclose anything further, I'm afraid. Please tell us where to find him and we'll be on our way." Hart was staying firm.

The woman sighed, making it obvious they were inconveniencing her. "You need to sign in before you go on the ward."

"Oh, we're not going on to the ward. If you can find Dr Randall and tell him to come and meet us, please," Hart said.

The woman stared at Hart, her mouth set into a straight line. Hart stood her ground. After a moment the silence was deafening. Swanson opened his mouth to interject.

"One minute, please," the woman said, saving him from having to think of something to say. She stood and left the office through a door behind her.

"Jesus christ. We're clearly not welcome," muttered Hart, rolling her eyes at Swanson. He raised an eyebrow in return.

"Don't you want to go on the ward to see what happened?" Swanson kept his voice low. He never knew who was listening, after all.

Hart shuddered. "I suppose we'll have to at some point, but I want that doctor with us before we enter. We might have arrested someone in there, for starters."

The door reopening made them both turn their heads. The woman had returned and ambled across the reception area without a word. She took her time in sitting down and sorting her chair into the correct position.

Swanson risked a glance at Hart. She was giving the lady an intense stare, her nostrils flared. He cleared his throat again and took a breath to suppress the laughter building up.

"Dr Randall isn't in, I'm afraid," the woman announced. For the first time, she smiled. A sickly sweet and sarcastic grin.

Swanson preferred her without a smile.

"Well, my colleague called this morning and was told he would be here to explain the situation that happened earlier this morning," Hart replied, struggling to keep her tone neutral.

"Oh, did he now? I'm so sorry you were told that. Which colleague was it? I'll make sure to have a word with them." She returned Hart's death stare easily.

"I'll find out the name when I get back to the station. If that was wrong, there must be another person here who can help? Another doctor?" Hart wasn't giving up easily.

The woman leaned back in her chair. She removed her glasses and breathed on them before answering.

"Not at the moment, I'm afraid. Dr Randall was on the ward at the time. He's our consultant psychiatrist. So it really is him you need to speak to."

"When will he be back?" Swanson cut in before Hart got any more agitated.

The receptionist wiped her glasses on her cardigan, and

shrugged. "I'm afraid I'm not sure."

"Has he gone home?" Swanson asked.

"No. I believe he had to visit someone urgently. I don't know exactly where. He was in a rush."

"OK. We will return tomorrow morning and expect that will be enough time to allow you to ensure Dr Randall will be available to answer our questions," Swanson said politely.

He opened the door and waited for Hart to walk through first. She glanced at him begrudgingly but took the hint. Once they were back in the corridor, Hart looked up at him and gaped.

"What the hell was that about?" she whispered, but as usual, she said it in such a way that it seemed much louder than her normal voice.

"Let's not talk about it here. Come on." He pushed past her and led the way back to the exit.

But he stopped at the stairs next to the exit and peered up at them. The red carpet continued up the steps to an open hallway at the top. Two doors were visible from his viewpoint. He walked to the bottom of the stairs and leaned to get a better view.

"What are you doing?" Hart whispered. Again, far louder than her usual voice.

A man's shout came from behind one door. It didn't sound particularly distressed. Was that all they'd heard earlier? A patient making noise? Swanson turned back around to face Hart.

"Nothing," he said, stepping off the stairs, "come on."

He opened up the steel exit and the blast of cool, fresh air hitting his skin was invigorating after the stifling warmth of the hospital. Swanson breathed it in deeply, but regret hit him immediately and he coughed and gagged. The air might be fresh, but there was a powerful stench of cow shit.

Hart laughed, despite her grievance with the reception woman. The pair crunched over the gravel in silence, each one lost in their own thoughts. It wasn't until they were in the car, doors closed, that Hart spoke.

"So, that was…strange," she said, her eyes fixated on the steering wheel but her mind appearing to be much further away as she assessed what had just happened.

"Yep. Very. She actually reminded me of my old English teacher. I never liked her either. Horrible old bag." He shuddered and pulled his seatbelt across his chest.

Hart did the same, started the engine and cranked up the dial for the heating. "Yeah, she was a bit *matronly*, wasn't she? Any thoughts on why she would want to stop us investigating such a dangerous incident?"

"She's possibly just a jobsworth, I guess. But there's definitely a weird vibe to this place, and she didn't exactly help with that." Swanson rubbed his hand against his beard.

Hart looked away to check the coast was clear before reversing out. Swanson stole the opportunity to slide his hand over and turn the heating back down. She turned back, oblivious to his actions, and rolled out of the Adrenna car park.

"It's haunted," she said, her face dark.

Swanson snorted. "OK. And how do you know that it's haunted?"

"Because I'm a better detective than you. I did my research and read about the hospital before we came," she replied in a smug tone.

"Ooh, ouch. Bit low when I was in hospital getting diagnosed with a bloody tumour." Swanson threw her a mock look of hurt.

"Pfft. Excuses, excuses, Detective Inspector Swanson. Don't think I'm letting you off that easily because of something as small as a tumour." She gave him a sly side glance and grinned.

"So what makes you think it's haunted?" Swanson asked again as Hart pulled onto the dirt track that led away from the hospital and back to the city.

"So, for starters, look at the place." She waved a hand in the general direction of the hospital.

Swanson didn't disagree. The place looked like the perfect haunted psychiatric hospital from an old horror film.

"Plus, from what I read online there's been loads of reports of ghosts. And not only from patients but from staff, too," she said as if staff were more reliable than the patients.

A few months ago Swanson might have agreed, but that wasn't his experience recently. Summer certainly wouldn't agree.

Who was that guy she was having breakfast with?

"I didn't think you were the type to believe in ghosts," Swanson said, pushing Summer out of his thoughts.

"Oh, yeah. My aunt's pub was haunted. It was mainly in the spare room." She shuddered. "The building had the *strangest* atmosphere, like Adrenna does. And she had all sorts happen. The lights would turn on and off-"

"Ooh, scary electrical faults." Swanson teased.

"-and so would the telly. They'd hear footsteps running up and down in the hall and heavy breathing," Hart carried on, ignoring Swanson's interjection. "Once a glass randomly smashed on its own. Just sitting there on the bar and it smashed!"

Swanson laughed. "Ghosts aren't real, Hart! Don't be a

wimp."

"Uh huh, you keep telling yourself that. I'm gonna bring you to my aunt's pub one day and then you'll believe me. Did you not feel the creepy vibe at Adrenna?"

He shrugged. "It felt weird. Who are these ghosts that supposedly haunt it?"

"Well, the original doctor who ran the hospital was called Brian Stockport. He actually died *inside* the hospital itself a couple of decades ago. He took over the hospital following privatisation of the social care system in the eighties. A patient murdered him, according to Wikipedia anyway. This patient stabbed him to death."

Swanson whistled. "Ouch. Murdered by those he was trying to help, eh? So, now the good doctor haunts the corridors, does he?"

"So some people will tell you. But that's not the strangest part." her smug smile was back.

"Go on. Spit it out," Swanson said in exasperation.

"His son died there, too. He was stabbed to death by a different patient ten years later."

"What?" Swanson turned to look at her, but he could tell when Hart was taking the piss out of him. She was deadly serious.

She nodded as the car flew down the winding country lanes at sixty miles an hour. "That's weird, I know. But again, not *as* weird as finding out they were both murdered in the same room!" She gleaned at him, proud of her trump card. "Loads of patients and staff have reported seeing either the older doctor or his son walking around the top floor of the hospital."

Swanson didn't respond, but took a moment to gather his thoughts. He didn't believe in ghosts or anything else supernatural. But even he had to admit it was a strange story.

"It's probably not true. Anyone can write anything on the internet. We need the records," he thought out loud.

Hart shrugged. "I wasn't sure either, but now I've been inside, I believe every word."

"Do you still want to go back tomorrow?" he asked.

Hart was quiet for a moment as she handled the roundabout which led to the city centre. Swanson gripped the handle above the door.

"Yep. I want to see that old bag again. I miss her already." She grinned and Swanson laughed. "What about you?"

"Me? I'm not the one who's scared of the ghosts," he replied.

Hart was quiet for a moment. "I meant your head. Do you feel up to it?"

"Of course." Swanson said more snappily than he meant to. He regretted his tone instantly. An awkwardness descended, and the pair sat in silence for the remaining few minutes of the drive.

Swanson tried to ignore the ever-increasing burning pain in the back of his head. But by the time Hart pulled into the station and parked haphazardly in a corner space, he was desperate to take his pain killers.

"You hungry? I'll buy us some food," Swanson said as he rushed to unbuckle his seatbelt.

"I'm not hungry, but I accept your offer as an apology," Hart said, "you might want to set aside a food allowance though if you're gonna be even grumpier than usual while the doctors fix you up."

Swanson made a mental note to add on some sort of chocolate pudding for her as they left the car.

"Nice parking." Swanson nodded towards the vehicle, which

was parked at a severe angle.

Hart glanced behind her at the car and shrugged. "Yep. I did it on purpose."

"Oh, yeah. Course you did."

"Yeah, I did. No one's going to want to park next to an idiot who parks like that." She pointed at the car and grinned.

"At least you admit what you are." Swanson shrugged and strode away quickly.

"Where are you rushing off to?" Hart called out.

"Getting away from you," he yelled back as he reached the station door.

Once inside, he rushed through the security door again and down the corridor to the bathroom. He ignored other officers and slammed the bathroom door behind him. Thank god, it was empty. His head throbbed, and he grabbed the pills from deep in his trouser pocket. He swallowed two dry and leant against the wall. He took a deep breath and waited for them to kick in. Only a few seconds passed before the door to the bathroom swung open.

Swanson jumped off the wall and cleared his throat.

"Woah, everything OK?" Officer Graham Forest, a fairly inexperienced officer who was skinny as a rake, looked at him with concern.

"Yep. Great." Swanson nodded to him and walked back out into the corridor.

He did not need Forest to suspect anything was going on. The man wasn't known for subtlety. Though Forest was a nice guy and didn't mean to blab, he couldn't help it. He didn't have the brainpower to think through his thoughts before speaking.

But as Swanson left the bathroom, the corridor spun. The tiled floor moved upwards, straight out from under his feet and smacked him in the nose.

How the hell did the floor move?

"Swanson?" Forest's voice was far away, echoing in the distance. A drowned out ringing noise flooded Swanson's ears.

"It was the bloody floor. It smacked me in the face," Swanson murmured, "why did the floor move?"

"Stupid floor." Hart's voice cut through the ringing much louder than Forest's.

Swanson's eyes flew back open.

"Get up, Krypto. I need my sidekick. Come on. Up you get. Move your fat arse yourself please. I'm not superwoman."

With his eyes now open, Swanson saw he was lying on the floor in the corridor. The floor hadn't moved. He'd fallen somehow. Multiple hands were pulling at him, but he barely budged. Hart and Forest stood little chance of dragging his dead weight up off the floor. He took a breath, put his palms on the floor, and heaved himself up to his knees.

"Butt on floor, head between knees," ordered Hart. For once, he did as she asked.

"What's going on?" A sharp female voice cut through the noise.

Swanson took a breath, and the ringing decreased now he was sitting up. He looked up and spotted a blurry Detective Chief Inspector Murray striding down the corridor towards him. *Shit*.

"Why are you on the floor?" she asked in a neutral tone which didn't hint at either annoyance or concern. She probably didn't feel either.

"Er…" Swanson tried to say *'I'm fine',* but no words came out. His tongue felt thick in his mouth. He couldn't use it properly.

"He said the floor moved and hit him in the face, Sir." Forest piped up.

Great, thanks Forest.

"What? Are you OK or not, Swanson?" DCI Murray asked.

He managed a nod.

"Good. Go home if you're ill. Let me know if you need anything else. Hart, sort him out." Murray walked off. "I don't want to see you back at work until you're better, Swanson. You're responsible for him, Hart," she yelled without turning to look back.

15

Swanson

The dizziness had passed by the time DCI Murray reached her office door at the end of the hall. Swanson waved Hart and Forest away and the pair stepped back. Yet they continued to stare at him as if ready to pounce any second. He put his hand against the wall. The coolness of the paint felt good against his clammy skin.

He leant all of his weight against it and pushed himself up, shaking off the instability in his legs. He felt their worried eyes staring at him, and his cheeks burnt.

"I just had a dizzy spell. Clearly I haven't drunk enough water," he said, though his voice came out with a strangled tone.

"Forest, get Swanson a glass of water, please," Hart commanded in a tone that warranted no arguments.

Forest turned and rushed off in the opposite direction to DCI Murray, heading towards the kitchen a few doors down. Two officers were chatting as they made their way by. They fell silent upon seeing Swanson leaning against the wall, though one swift glance from Hart sent them scampering by without asking questions.

"I'm not going to tell you to rest, because I know you're not stupid enough *not* to realise that yourself. But I am telling you I'm going to drive you home," Hart said once the two officers were out of earshot.

"I can't leave my car here," Swanson said, although thinking of driving himself home made him groan internally.

"That's what taxis are for, you tight sod," Hart replied.

The pair heard footsteps, and turned to see Forest rushing down the hall with a glass of water, drops spilling out of it everywhere. Swanson suppressed a laugh. He hadn't seen Forest's gangly form *rush* anywhere before.

"Here." Forest presented the half empty glass with a deeply concerned expression.

"Thanks, Forest." Swanson took the glass and downed it in three gulps. The water eased the shaking sensation enough so he no longer needed to lean on the wall.

"Do you feel better?" Forest asked and took the empty glass from him.

"He's fine, Forest. Give him some space," Hart said. She gave him one of her special death stares.

Forest nodded and moved back a step.

Hart continued to glare at him.

"Er, I'll finish going to the loo." He eventually got the hint and hurried back into the men's bathroom.

"Come on." Hart put a hand on Swanson's arm.

"I'm fine." He shrugged her away.

"Shut-up, you are not fine." She pulled at his arm again until he stepped forward. "Come on."

She walked off and motioned for him to follow her. Swanson sighed, but did as she asked. He contemplated driving himself home. He was more stable now the water had done its job. Maybe he really was hungry and dehydrated. *Did he have breakfast?* The day was a blur. He thought back to that morning, preparing for the hospital. His stomach had felt full of nerves about the appointment with Dr Tiffin. He definitely hadn't had lunch. That must be the problem.

"I can see what you're thinking, and it's not happening," Hart called out without turning to look at him. "I already took your key when you were sitting on the floor."

Swanson stopped dead in his tracks and shoved his hands in each pocket, searching for the key.

"Seriously, Robin," he yelled down the corridor to her. "The last thing a dizzy person needs is your erratic, bloody driving."

Hart stopped too and turned to face him. She was grinning. "You've survived one trip with me already today. You can survive another."

He didn't know if he was more annoyed at Hart taking his keys, or at the sense of relief he felt she had taken the choice from him. He'd rather not be stuck at home without a car, and not even be able to check if it was OK. But really any car would be safer in a police station parking lot than in the driveway of his cottage. And it was safer without him driving it whilst so unwell. At least until he ate something.

They snuck out of the building through the rear fire doors, an exit that led straight to the car park and was supposed to be for emergencies only. But Swanson figured Murray would rather they took the back entrance than him causing any further scenes in front of people.

The air was muggy compared to the freshness of the morning. Or did it feel that way because he was still hot and clammy? He crossed the car park once again to Hart's badly parked

Astra. It was clear from the heavy air that more rain was on the way, and he wished it would hurry. Standing in the rain at that moment would have been lovely. He stood tall despite the tremour in his legs and forced each one to move in long strides.

Once in the car Hart reached out to turn up the heat, but glanced at him and decided against it. They fell into a comfortable silence this time. Hart didn't say a thing until she had to ask him for directions when they were a few streets away from Swanson's cottage. She'd visited twice before, but a sense of direction wasn't a strong point of hers, putting it mildly.

"Here you go, Sir," she said with a weird seated bow action as she pulled up on the curb outside of his home.

A calmness fell over Swanson at the sight of the wonky little cottage. He couldn't remember another time when he'd needed the silence of his own space more.

"Come on," Hart said, opening her car door.

Swanson's calmness dissipated.

"What are you doing?" he asked.

"I need to borrow your charger to make a call, then I'm gone, OK?" She raised her hands in the air as if being arrested.

"You're a liar." Swanson got out of the car too and headed towards his pale green door. It desperately needed repainting when he had a spare afternoon.

"No, genuinely, I thought I may as well get an update from the hospital on the woman who was attacked whilst I'm with you. It will save you the job of calling me later. You know, when you've tried to relax but got bored and decided to work again." She gave him a knowing look.

Swanson unwillingly agreed and let them both into the

cottage, which opened straight into the cosy, misshapen living room with its ancient sofa and low ceilings. He stooped as he entered the room.

"Mind your head." Swanson looked down at Hart, whose head cleared the threshold by at least half a foot. She rolled her eyes at his sarcasm.

"I suppose you want a coffee?" he asked.

"Do you actually have coffee in?" Her face lit up.

"Nope."

She let out an exaggerated sigh. "You're actually even more infuriating when you're sick. Where's your charger?"

He pointed to an extension cable with a mess of wires in the corner of the room, half hidden by the sofa.

"That's a bloody fire hazard." Hart tutted. She walked over and perched on the edge of the sofa, reaching over the arm to grab the charger. She pulled it through a mass of wires, shaking her head and tutting some more.

"I'll give it a minute to charge," she said once she'd sorted the charger wire and plonked the phone on the arm of the sofa.

Swanson flicked off his loafers and sat on the barely used armchair across from her. She was in his usual space. He closed his eyes and allowed the annoyance of not being able to sit on his sofa spot to wash over him.

"Stop staring at me. I'm fine," he grumbled.

"Well, you're not though, you have a tumour," she said simply.

"Yes, well. Thanks for that reminder. It helped a lot."

She turned her body to face him and gave him a serious look.

"You're welcome. There's no point in it being an elephant in the room. You need to get used to it so you can beat it. I assume that's right, anyway. Sounds right, doesn't it? Spit it out. What are the next steps to make it go away?"

She wouldn't give up until she knew the full story. He'd seen her use the same technique with witnesses and criminals a hundred times. It was partly what made her so good at the job. He sighed and shuffled back in his chair, unsure how to get comfy on the unfamiliar piece of furniture.

"I need a biopsy first to see how it's growing. It might be benign, or it might be cancerous," he admitted. The words felt strange. Like he was lying, or dreaming, or as if someone else should say them.

She nodded. "So, when is the biopsy?"

He shrugged. "I don't know yet. They'll call me to let me know soon."

"You need to tell Murray asap so you can be available last minute for it." She fell silent and fiddled with a piece of hair. "Do you want me to come with you? I can take the piss out of you while you wait. It might make you feel better."

Swanson stared at her. "Come with me? To the hospital?" he repeated slowly, as if he misunderstood.

"Yes, Swanson. Come with you. Support you. You understand that, right? Actually, you might need someone to drive you home anyway with the anaesthetic and all that."

Swanson paused and looked out of the small window of his front room. It still wasn't raining. "I can get a taxi there and back."

"Pfft. Yeah right. You're as tight as a duck's arse! That would cost you a tenner at least and that's just for one way."

That *was* expensive. She had a point.

"I'm not even that tight. Just because I don't spend hundreds on one bloody dog handbag." He pointed to her leather bag with the little dog symbol that he knew indicated some sort of expensive designer handbag.

"Whatever. Let me know the date and I'll be there. I'm not giving you a choice." She crossed her arms like a stubborn toddler.

"Fine, if you insist." Swanson was too hungry to argue.

He stood back up and walked into the kitchen to see what snacks he had. He rammed a couple of pork pies and some ham into his mouth. Then pulled out a carton of chunky chicken soup and swiftly emptied it into a bowl. As he waited for the microwave to ping, he dug out the box of chocolates from his cupboard that he had meant to give to Summer a few weeks ago and went back through to the living room.

"Here." He shoved the chocolates onto Hart's lap, along with the rest of the pork pies.

She grinned. "Thanks!"

"Yeah, well, I'll need to keep your blood sugar up if you're going to keep fussing over me all the time. You'll be bloody intolerable otherwise."

"Soo, all I heard there was *thank you for being a great mate. I love you and appreciate you.*" She peered up at him, still perched in his favourite spot.

"Yep. That's what I said." He went back into the kitchen to fetch his soup and some bread.

He heard Hart through the open door which adjoined the living room and kitchen. There was no room for a hallway in the cottage.

"Hi, Forest. just checking for an update on the hospital worker who's... er... in hospital?" She fell silent as she waited for a response. Swanson dipped the butterless bread in the soup and thrust it into his mouth before drinking the rest of the bowl. Living alone meant no need for manners. He placed the bowl in the empty sink and made his way back into the living room to resign himself to the armchair.

"Want a sandwich?" he mouthed to Hart.

She shook her head. "Stable? OK," she replied to Forest.

"Is she a nurse?" Swanson asked in a loud whisper.

"Did we find out if she was a nurse or a doctor?" Hart asked.

Swanson heard the rumbling of Forest's voice, but not what he was saying. But as Hart's eyes widened, he realised it wasn't good news. She glanced at Swanson, but quickly looked away. Her usually peachy cheeks suddenly quite a shade lighter.

"She was a what? Are you sure? Get me her name, now. How do we not know it yet? OK, I need to go. Get that name to me asap." She hung up and continued to stare at the floor, as if deep in thought.

He almost didn't want to know. "Are you going to tell me what's wrong?"

She slowly raised her head. She was worryingly pale. "Have you spoken to Summer recently?"

"Yesterday. But then I saw her this morning having breakfast with... a friend. Didn't speak to her, though. Why?" Swanson asked. *Who was that bloody guy?*

He suddenly realised what Hart had asked him. *Why* she must be asking him.

His head snapped up. "Why, Hart?" he demanded.

She swallowed. "That woman who was stabbed... she was an advocate. A visiting one, not a usual member of staff."

Swanson tugged his phone out of his trouser pocket, his hands sweating. He ignored the new wave of dizziness rushing through him. His adrenaline pumping. He ignored all other thoughts and focused on dialling Summer's number. It absolutely could not be her. He'd just seen her, how could it be? But her phone went straight to voicemail.

16

Swanson

A grim mixture of panic and anger curdled and settled within Swanson's chest. He stood up, fighting away the dizziness that threatened to overcome him. His face hot with anger.

"It went straight to voicemail. How do we not know the name yet?" He tried to keep his voice calm, but he was sounding more panicky with each word.

Hart's own face paled. She stood to face him. "Someone will know. Wait one minute. Even if it is her, Forest said she was stable, OK? Stay calm."

She picked up her phone and quickly tapped something before holding it to her ear. Swanson went into the kitchen and redialled Summer's mobile. It went straight to voicemail again. His hands squeezed into fists as he walked back into the living room, his nails digging into his palms.

"Forest is going to find out the name of the victim asap. Apparently the nurse at Adrenna didn't know the name when they called it in because she was a new advocate to them, but they had it recorded in the visitor log and were going to let us know. I'll go to the hospital in the meantime. She's still unconscious, but if they've found it out then they'll tell us her name if we're face to face."

Swanson marched over to his shoes and shoved his feet into them. "I'm coming with you."

"Jesus, Swanson. Fine. I'll bloody find you a bed and leave you there," she muttered as she stormed past him to the front door. Swanson followed right on her heel and slammed the door behind them.

"Lock it." Hart jerked her head toward his front door.

"Shit, keys." He ran back inside to grab them and nearly tripped on the threshold on his way back out.

Hart was already in her car by the time he'd locked up. He rushed around to the passenger side to join her in the vehicle. The adrenaline made him feel more focused than he had done all day. He had Summer to focus on now. And he was on his way to help. It was going to be OK. The tumour could go fuck itself at that moment.

He hit redial and reached her voicemail again. All the times he could have asked Summer for a drink ran through his mind, and how silly it was that he didn't, just because she'd been busy the one time he'd asked.

They didn't talk on the drive. Hart knew him well enough to leave him alone with his thoughts. She pulled into the hospital fifteen minutes later and parked on the grass near the entrance. They jumped out and raced inside to the reception desk. People lined the waiting area, but moved out of the way as soon as they saw Swanson striding through. The young brunette on the reception desk watched him approach with wide eyes, not taking them off him once.

"Hi, high dependency unit, please?" he panted, struggling to catch his breath.

She pointed over her shoulder and belted out directions, clearly having said the same thing a million times before. The pair rushed down the corridor and arrived at the lifts breathless. A few minutes later they were on the right floor, and Swanson stopped abruptly, almost causing Hart to careen into the back of him.

Aaron Walker was sitting outside the ward. He wore his nurse's uniform still, and was leaning forward with his head in his hands. Swanson recognised his ridiculous, thick black hair and massive earring from interviewing him a couple of months back about Lucy Clark. Next to him was a lady in her sixties with sallow skin and thin grey hair which fell around her shoulders. It was Summer's mum. Swanson had met her once before. The man Swanson had seen with Summer in the cafe sat next to her. So whoever he was, he knew Summer and her mum well enough to be sitting here. His eyes were also swollen, though he looked more angry than upset.

"Jesus, Swanson," Hart said in between breaths. "Don't just stop like that!"

She came out from behind him, but fell silent when she saw Aaron and Summer's mum. Hart was with Swanson when he met both of them, and she knew what their presence outside the ward signalled. Aaron looked up at the sound of Hart's voice. Beads of sweat gathered on Swanson's forehead, but he wiped them away. He needed to focus.

"Officer Swanson?" Aaron stood, a confused look on his face. "Er… Not sure if you remember me, Aaron Walker?"

"Yes, yes. I remember you. I heard an advocate was attacked and Summer isn't picking up her phone?" He knew the likelihood of Summer not being in the ward was pretty much zero, but he asked regardless. He needed to hear someone say it.

Aaron nodded solemnly. He moved away from Summer's mum, who hadn't looked over once, and said in a low voice. "I was there. I saw the whole thing. A patient attacked her with some sort of glass or razor. They hit her in the neck. That's Summer's mum." He motioned towards the woman with his head. Swanson glanced over at her. She didn't look much like Summer. She looked as though she'd fall over if you breathed too hard near her.

"And that's her brother." Aaron nodded over to the angry man with swollen eyes.

A sense of relief hit Swanson at hearing the man was her brother, though it was short-lived when he remembered why they were all there. The man looked younger than Summer. He had her fair hair and a straight nose. He remembered her telling him about a younger brother. *Was it Dave? Declan?*

"Have you had an update on how she's doing?" Swanson forced his attention back to Aaron. His breath stuck in his chest as he waited for the answer.

"They've operated on her already and have closed the wound. They let us in to see her for a few minutes earlier. She's stable, but she's not awake yet. They wanted to check all of her equipment and stats so we came to wait out here."

Swanson closed his eyes briefly and let out the breath he'd been holding. "And where's Joshua?"

Aaron raised his eyebrows. Was he surprised that Swanson knew the child's name? How close were Aaron and Summer, anyway?

"He's at school," Aaron answered, "but his dad is going to pick him up."

Hart put a hand on Swanson's arm and interjected. "Thanks, Mr Walker."

Aaron nodded and hesitated as if he was going to say something else, but he walked off back to his chair. It was rare for anyone to not do as Hart asked straight away.

"I've got a missed call from the station. I'll be back in a minute," Hart said in a low voice and walked off down the corridor they had just come from.

Swanson leaned against the wall, his mind racing. Whilst he had been in the very same hospital, worrying about himself, Summer was about to turn up fighting for her life and he didn't even know it. Poor Joshua was going to be confused and worried. Then he realised what Aaron said.

He shot off the wall and stormed over to Aaron, who looked up at him in surprise and shrank back in his chair. A reaction Swanson was used to in response to him getting too close.

"You said you were there?" Swanson said.

Summer's mum still didn't look at him. She was staring into space. Her eyes were vacant. But he felt the brother's eyes on him, though he said nothing.

"Er… Yes. I work there now. It's my new job," Aaron said, "or was, anyway. It's a strange place. Not sure I'll stick around."

"Will you come and give a statement?" Swanson asked.

"Sure, do you need me now, though? I kind of wanted to stay here for now, with Summer." He pointed over to the entrance of the ward.

"I only want to know what happened. Let's talk over here." Swanson moved over to a quiet corner of the corridor away from Summer's family. Aaron followed closely behind him.

"So, talk me through what happened briefly now, and we'll take a proper statement later," he said in a low voice.

"Well, it was all a bit of a blur, if I'm honest. I walked on to the ward. I wasn't supposed to be in, but I was covering the early shift for a colleague. So I went to Ward C, straight into the living area, and a patient next to Summer jumped up and went crazy. He stabbed her in the neck with a razor blade he'd stolen from somewhere. There was blood everywhere. I set the alarm off on my belt and ran over to her."

"Why did he stab her?" Swanson asked.

Aaron shrugged. "No idea. He's a fairly new patient and still under supervision."

"Clearly not intensive enough supervision," Swanson said.

Aaron didn't respond.

"Did you notice anything else? Anything unusual?" Swanson asked.

"That's it, really. I held the wound and stopped the blood flow, and a different nurse called an ambulance." He rubbed his face with his hands again.

It was only now that Swanson noticed Aaron's eyes were bloodshot too, and blood stained the bottom of his top. Summer's blood. Swanson felt sick.

"I really thought she was a goner," Aaron whispered.

A furious rage sat within Swanson's chest. Someone was going to pay for hurting Summer. He heard the sharp tap of heels against tiles and turned away from Aaron. Hart was on her way towards them.

"That was the hospital. Dr Randall is back," she said.

17

The Servant

I watched out of the ward window and waited for the officer's red car to pull up. They didn't take long once I'd given the order. I watched the woman park up and leave her car in a slanted position in the middle of the gravel. And I repeated the registration number until I had it committed to memory.

I was pleased it was the same officers as earlier. They didn't stay in the car this time, and instead exited as soon as they'd parked up. The man strode over the gravel path, with the woman barely able to keep up with him, stumbling over the gravel again in her heels.

I'd been right in thinking she was no good for the Devil. He wouldn't like her demeanour at all. She wasn't worthy of Him, far too brash and common. But the man would do nicely.

He moved slowly, despite his big strides, like he had purpose to each step. His eyes scanned the area and took in every detail. His thoroughness was clear. The Devil would like that. It was a superb skill for a protector to have.

Plus, I knew he had a tumour. The Devil had told me.

So I didn't even need to feel any guilt about killing him. He was dying anyway. But we couldn't wait around. Tumours can make people weak. He needed to be strong like he was now. I had to weaken him enough to get him into the chamber. In a one-on-one fight, he would easily overpower me.

I'll explain to him why beforehand, maybe he'll understand. Maybe he'll think I'm crazy. Most people would. But the shadows of the Devil have not touched those people as they lay in bed. Most people think a simple duvet will protect them from any monsters.

You can't see the shadow looking at you in the dark. But trust me, it's there, and it can see you.

18

Swanson

Swanson was grateful that Hart had put her foot down and sped through the city. The heavens finally opened again as the city merged into countryside and he watched as large raindrops bounced off the bonnet. But it didn't slow her down. Instead, she reached Adrenna in record time. He'd always had the feeling that Hart didn't like Summer much, but maybe she cared about her more than he realised.

The building loomed before them in no time at all, looking even more depressing against the grey skies and torrential rain. Hart threw her car into a random spot on the gravel, and they stormed across the car park and down the side of the building to the steel door they'd used earlier that morning.

Swanson pressed the buzzer on the intercom and counted to three before pressing it again. His hands rolled into tight fists. He heard Hart's quick footsteps behind him. She'd caught up to him. He glanced over at her. She was giving him a wary glare.

"Let me do the talking," she said, pulling her hood up tight over her face.

He shook his head. "No way." He pulled his own hood over his head. His trousers were already sticking to his legs.

Hart leant right against the wall, trying to get out of the way of the colossal rain drops. "You're too angry, you know you are. You shouldn't be here, really. Murray would flip."

"I don't care. Nobody knows I have anything to do with Summer, other than interviewing her the other month. And to be fair to them, I don't. Not really. The other times we met were to talk about her brother mainly." He turned away from her. "I can still be professional. Don't worry. I won't lose my temper."

"You will if they say something stupid," she muttered.

He raised an eyebrow and heaved his shoulders. "They better not say anything stupid then."

"Murray *is* gonna be pissed when she finds out you didn't go home. Plus, I'm pretty sure this level of stress isn't good for a brain tumour."

Swanson ignored her and pushed the bell again. Nobody spoke, but the buzzer sounded this time, and the steel door clicked to signal it was unlocked. Swanson pushed it open and stalked down the corridor into the reception area.

"Dr Randall will be with you in one moment," the old witch said from behind her reception desk as soon as he walked in. Hart was right behind him, with a face that said she was disappointed she would not get to argue.

"You can take a seat if your trousers aren't too wet," the receptionist continued, though Swanson swore she was hiding a smirk.

Neither of them moved. Swanson knew he looked surly, but he didn't care. He stood rooted to the spot and stared in the woman's direction. He wasn't taking any shit this time.

It only took a minute for a man to appear from behind the reception desk. Dr Randall, Swanson assumed. His height matched Swanson's six feet, though he was much skinnier with a bean pole figure and a head of floppy brown hair. He smiled at them both as he strode over, his teeth slightly crooked. At least he seemed friendlier than the receptionist.

"Hi, guys, hi. How are you both? I'm Dr Randall." He put forward a large and bony hand to shake Swanson's. "Lovely to meet you."

Swanson took the doctor's hand. "Detective Inspector Alex Swanson," he said curtly. He pulled his eyes away to stop himself from staring at the largest pair of glasses he'd ever seen. Dr Randall held the same hand out to Hart, who took it and introduced herself in the same curt fashion. Rain always annoyed her. She'd be in a mood until she was dry again.

"Follow me, please. My office is right down here and we can have a bit of a chat about the recent incident. Such a terrible accident." He shook his head and strode off back down the side of the reception desk.

Swanson clenched his jaw. It certainly wasn't an *accident.* Dr Randall unlocked a heavy wooden door and held it open as the pair walked through. Behind the door was another corridor which led round to the left of the building and followed behind the initial hallway.

"I'm sorry to have to bring you all the way down here because of a patient. I'm sure you have other criminals to catch that aren't safely cared for in a locked facility." Dr Randall threw them both an apologetic glance.

The pair said nothing. Swanson clenched his jaw harder. It might be harder to stay calm than he thought. They walked past a few more doors. Swanson glanced at the sign on each one. *G Randall. B Stockport. Store room. J Randall.* Dr Randall opened the last one and led them inside.

"This is me." He smiled, and once again held the door for them.

"Thank you," said Hart.

Swanson still kept his jaw clenched. This guy was way too polite. It was unsettling somehow. He surveyed the office. It was a mess. Boxes of books and paper files lined both walls, and a desk full of paperwork was positioned at the back of the room in front of a window. He glanced at the books.

Neuropsychiatry and the mind.

A History of Mental Health.

The Devil of Adrenna.

Dr Randall took a seat on the other side of his messy desk and motioned for them to each take a seat across from him. The window was behind his desk, with blinds that were half closed and prevented too much light seeping through. To the right of his desk was another door. Swanson stared at it. A door there made no sense to the layout of the building. Where the hell would it lead to? Dr Randall grabbed some papers and shoved them into a desk drawer. Swanson couldn't keep his mouth shut any longer.

"So where were you when we visited earlier?" he asked with no effort made to keep the annoyance out of his voice.

"Er... we had an incident on the ward, I'm afraid. A patient attacked another patient." He removed his glasses and wiped them on his white coat. "It's not been an enjoyable week, unfortunately. I had to declare the ward unsafe and couldn't allow any visitors."

"We were told you were out. Unreachable," Swanson said.

Dr Randall swallowed. His unusually large Adam's apple

bobbing up and down. He recovered quickly, flashing another big smile. "Out? Oh no, I practically live here," he said with a nervous chuckle, "but I was busy dealing with the aftermath and making sure everybody was safe. Glenda must have gotten the wrong end of the stick."

"Glenda?" Hart said.

"Yes. The receptionist." He nodded again. Christ, he was like one of those annoying nodding dogs people used to put in their cars, the ones with the stupid big grins.

"Oh, I see. She didn't exactly introduce herself," Hart said.

"Oh, apologies. She can be blunt. The patients are very important to her. She means well." Dr Randall set his glasses back on his face and leant forward in his seat. "How is the advocate? Such a lovely woman."

"She's in hospital and might die," Swanson said. He felt Hart's eyes on him as she glanced over. She wasn't approving of his bluntness, then.

"Oh, dear! That is awful." Dr Randall sat back in his chair.

"For now, she's alive," Hart butted in before Swanson responded. "Can you tell me what happened, please?"

"Well, yes. Of course. I was doing my rounds, visiting the wards and making sure all is OK. Summer was sitting next to Andy when I entered Ward C. I thought I'd say hello, you know, like I usually do. I like to make everyone feel welcome. So I walked over to Summer and Andy and as I got there he jumped up and hit her-"

"*Hit* her?" Swanson interrupted.

"Well, that's what I thought he did. I rushed forward to restrain him and he cut my hand." He stopped to pull up a sleeve and show them a bandaged left hand. "I was quite close anyway, you see. I heard the alarms going off and saw blood. That's when I realised she'd been more badly hurt than I thought. It wasn't until a couple of other nurses came running over to help me pin Andy down I saw how much blood there was. I helped get Andy to the quiet room and locked the door. When I returned I saw the razor blade on the floor. I swiped it up and by this time sirens could be heard and a nurse, Aaron, was looking after Summer."

"Are you a qualified doctor?" Swanson asked.

Dr Randall frowned. "Sorry?"

"Are you a qualified medical doctor?" Swanson repeated through gritted teeth.

"Yes, of course. All psychiatrists study medicine, if that's what you're asking." Dr Randall looked perplexed.

"Why didn't you let the support staff handle the patient, like they're trained to do, and you, as a doctor, help the bleeding woman?" Swanson asked.

"I really didn't know how serious it was." Dr Randall's voice was suddenly much higher.

"Where's the patient now?" Hart butted in again.

"He's still in solitary confinement. He seems much calmer, but I have not deemed it safe to release him yet."

"Can we speak to him?" Hart asked.

He shook his head. "Not at the minute. He's really not very well and so he is still dangerous at present. Plus, he would need an appropriate adult at least. I'll call you as soon as he's calmed down. But I can tell you that when I spoke to him earlier, he said he couldn't remember the incident."

"He couldn't remember at all?" Hart asked.

Dr Randall shook his head. "Not hurting her. He remembered sitting next to her, and being thrown into the confinement room. But the attack is a blind spot."

"Do you have cameras on the ward?" Hart asked.

"Yes, but where this incident happened is also a blind spot, unfortunately."

"Can you at least show us the ward so we can see where the incident happened?" Swanson asked, standing up before Dr Randall could answer.

"Yes, of course." The doctor jumped up despite looking like he'd rather do anything but.

He stood and led them back through the corridor to a door at the other end. Swanson hadn't noticed there was another door here. It led into the initial hallway with the steel door. And the stairs to the first floor were in front of them.

"Just up here," the doctor said as he leaped up the stairs. He had an annoying way of bouncing rather than walking, with his shoulders hunched over. Swanson followed more cautiously, with Hart right behind him.

At the top of the stairs, there were three doors. Dr Randall led them to the one on the right. He peered through the glass and fiddled with a key ring that was attached to his belt.

"Before we enter, I need you to know that this is the ward where our most volatile patients live. This is the ward they enter when they first arrive, and we don't know them very well yet. You must be vigilant and stay with me. I have my alarm to call for help if needed."

Swanson glanced over at Hart in surprise.

"Thanks for the heads up, but I think we'll be OK with the three of us together, Doctor," she said.

The two of them entered the ward behind Dr Randall. They stepped forward as he made sure he'd locked the door behind them. Swanson squeezed his hands into fists to control the urge to storm around the ward. If he wanted answers for

Summer, he would have to stay calm and investigate properly. As he entered the ward he saw one patient sitting on the sofa, staring into space. Another walked in circles, muttering to himself.

His heart sank. This was not the best place to be looking for answers.

But as he gazed around the rest of the ward, a bolt of recognition hit him in the gut. Because for the second time that day, two blank eyes of an old stranger stared straight at him.

19

Swanson

Swanson's stomach churned violently. He grabbed Hart's arm to get her attention.

"What?" she asked, craning her neck to see what he was looking at.

He turned to her. "That man with cataracts or whatever, white eyes, I saw him earlier, in the supermarket car park."

She turned back to him and frowned. "What bloody man with cataracts?"

"There!" Swanson turned to point.

But he was pointing at an empty space. The man had disappeared.

"He was right there." He glared at the wide open living area in front of him. The man was here somewhere. Dr Randall appeared next to them.

"Like I said, I'm afraid you won't get much out of the patients in this ward. I sent the staff who saw the incident home. You know, to rest." He gave them a solemn look.

"I saw an older patient with eye problems. His eyes were completely white. Who is he?"

The doctor paused and looked away, scratching his head.

"I... er... I don't actually know. I don't think we have any patients with such serious eye problems. Definitely no one who is blind. Unless we've had some sort of emergency admitted by another doctor, but even then I would be made aware."

"He was right there." Swanson pointed to the corner of the ward where he'd seen the man.

"Oh... er... Ok. Let's ask a nurse, shall we? This way, please."

The doctor led them to an office which took up the left-hand side of the ward. Most of the front wall was actually a large window that you could see directly into with ease. It must make it easy for nurses to sit there watching patients.

Dr Randall fiddled with his keys again. Swanson noticed his hand shook a little, and he struggled to get the right key. Swanson glanced around the ward before entering to check again for the old man, but he was nowhere to be seen. Dr Randall finally found the right key and held open the door to allow them to pass through.

"Wait inside here a moment, please," he instructed before closing the door and heading back onto the ward.

"Where the hell is he going?" Hart murmured and peered through the window to watch him. "I don't like being locked in small rooms."

"Hopefully to find the old man," Swanson said.

"Oh yeah, the one with no eyes?" She turned to face him. One hand on her hip.

"Not no eyes! White eyes."

"OK, OK. White eyes. It's still weird as fuck, Swanson. Do brain tumours cause hallucinations?"

"No." Swanson felt the heat in his face rising and clenched

his jaw tight. Did they cause bloody hallucinations?

"OK. Don't get mad at me for putting it out there. You'd ask me the same thing if I was seeing weird things like that."

He turned away from her and looked through the glass to watch out for Dr Randall instead. He spotted him walking across the ward towards them with a nurse in tow. She couldn't have been older than 25. The top of her head only reached Dr Randall's chest. She looked up and her wide eyes met his. Swanson smiled and turned away, not wanting to intimidate her before he'd even said hello.

They entered the office a moment later with Dr Randall still wearing his ridiculous big grin. She followed behind him with her head down, playing nervously with her hair.

"This is Jenna Twiggs, one of our excellent nurses on shift today," Dr Randall announced, as if they were from a quality of care inspection team. "I'll wait outside and watch the patients for you, Jenna. Give me a shout if any of you need anything." He left swiftly, closing the office door behind him.

"Hi Jenna." Swanson swallowed and forced a smile again. It didn't feel natural, but she gave him a small smile back so he couldn't be doing too badly. "I'm Detective Inspector Swanson, and this is my colleague, Detective Inspector Hart."

"Hi," her voice was soft, not unlike Summer's.

"We're here because of the stabbing that occurred this morning," Hart interjected like a bloody foghorn. Swanson sighed inwardly.

"Oh, I wasn't here, I'm afraid. I wasn't on shift." Jenna continued to curl her hair around one finger.

"Have you heard anything about what happened?" Hart persisted.

"Erm… yes. That Andy got the advocate in the neck with

some sort of razor." She lowered her head. "I really like her. She cares so much about the patients. Is she going to be OK?"

"She should be." Swanson nodded. "Can I ask, is there an older patient on this ward who has a disability concerning his eyes?"

She gave him a dazed look of bewilderment. "Disability concerning his eyes? Do you mean blind?"

"Possibly. He is around 70 or 80 years old, with a white beard, and has white eyes." Swanson watched as the colour drained from her face. Her head snapped round to look out of the window and into the ward.

"Where did you see him?" She demanded, suddenly standing to get a better look out of the window.

"In that corner." Swanson pointed to the far side of the ward. "Then he seemed to... vanish."

Jenna's shoulders relaxed, and she turned to him. "No. I have no idea who you're talking about. Sorry. Do you have any other questions?"

He shook his head.

"OK. I better get back to giving out the meds. It was lovely to meet you."

"Lovely to meet you too, Jenna Twiggs," Swanson said softly.

As soon as the door was closed behind her, he turned to Hart, who still stood with one hand on her hip. "Did you see her reaction?"

"She got up to look out the window, Swanson. She was trying to see what the hell you were talking about. Come on, let's go find the good doctor and get out of here. It's messing with your bloody head."

He opened his mouth to argue, but something about the look on her face stopped him. She'd already asked once about hallucinations. He didn't need her thinking that was actually true.

And he'd seen how the nurse had jumped up to look for the man. She knew who he was talking about, didn't she?

20

Swanson

Swanson huffed as he hauled himself into Hart's car and slammed the door. Visiting the ward had proved pointless. He'd not found one scrap of information, and could happily never visit that damn hospital again. Now all he could think about was the old man. The nurse obviously knew who he'd meant. The mention of him had terrified her.

"So, what do you think of the good doctor?" asked Hart.

"He's too..." Swanson racked his brain for the right word. He wasn't going to mention the old man again to Hart. He didn't need to give her any more evidence that he was losing his mind.

"Chirpy?" Hart suggested.

"Yes, definitely. But there's something else." He turned to gaze out of the window, willing his brain to focus.

"Happy?" Hart tried again. "You know how you hate overly cheerful people."

"Well, yes. If you were responsible for a patient that might have murdered an innocent woman, when you were standing right next to her, would you be *that* happy?" He glanced over at Hart, who threw her seatbelt on.

"He seemed more nervous to me, and overly friendly. Certainly nicer than Glenda. He doesn't seem the type to have dealings with the police often." She clicked the seatbelt into position, sat back, and chewed her lip. Her 'deep in thought' face.

"Yeah, maybe that's all it is."

"He was probably worried we'd shut him down or something." Hart shrugged and checked the empty car park was clear twice before rolling off the gravel. A remnant of her paranoia after hitting a bollard a few months ago while reversing out of a factory car park.

"Mmm." Swanson shuffled back in his seat and returned to gazing out of the window. He would've killed for five minutes of peace to think things through.

"Where am I going, anyway? Shall I take you home?" She asked as they reached the dirt road for the fourth time that day. He was sick of this road. Of Adrenna. Of not having any peace. He rubbed the deep throb at the back of his head.

"No. I'm feeling loads better. Let's go back to the station. I'll drive home." The call of his quiet cottage was too hard to resist.

"Are you sure?" He felt her eyeing him suspiciously.

He nodded. "I'm sensible enough to pull over if I need to, Ma'am."

"You look better. Not as deathly grey as you looked this morning. Still butt ugly, though." She chuckled at her own joke.

"Hilarious, Robin."

"I am indeed, Krypto."

The traffic in the city was quiet. It was the deceiving calm right before the rush hour storm began at 4pm. Hart continued to eyeball him once they'd reached the police station car park and walked over to his black Audi. She passed him his car keys slowly, as if about to change her mind. He snatched them from her before she could. Wrestling a female coworker in the car park wouldn't be a good look for him.

"I'm going to call you in thirty minutes flat," she said before taking a step back to watch him as if he were a patient from Adrenna.

He nodded and jumped into his car. He threw an over the top wave her way as he rolled out of the station car park. She stuck her middle finger up. Being back in his own car gave him a sense of control that had been severely lacking throughout the day. In particular, the ability to control the heater.

Summer crossed his mind. Should he go back to the hospital? Would she even want him there? He couldn't very well sit next to her mum. What would he say to her? He knew her mum didn't know about their meetings to discuss finding Eddie, as she had no idea Summer was looking for him.

So he raced to his cottage instead, beating a further downfall of rain as he pulled up on his drive. He rushed inside and slammed the door behind him, not bothering to lock it, and kicked off his loafers at the bottom of the staircase.

The cottage was cold having sat in the low December temperatures empty and so with no heating on. He flicked on the central heating, then went to the kitchen to fill a pint glass with tap water. The water was bracing as it ran down his throat. He couldn't remember ever buying a pint glass in his life, and yet somehow he had half a shelf full of them in his cupboard.

The old floorboards creaked as he walked over to the sofa

and took a seat where Hart perched earlier that day. Happy that he was sitting back where he belonged. He pulled out his laptop from underneath the ancient coffee table, which was yet another thing he didn't remember buying.

Hart said that the original doctor of Adrenna died 30 years ago, and his son died 20 years ago. Both were stabbed to death in the same room, and both were stabbed by a patient. Then there was the old man that nobody else wanted to admit to seeing. Who the hell was he, and how was he connected?

He blinked hard and held back a yawn. Christ, he'd already had a nap in the car park that morning, and in Hart's car on the first drive to Adrenna. The exhaustion was a killer. His tumour hadn't even caused tiredness prior to today. Maybe it was getting bigger.

Either way, sleep would have to wait. He needed to do something useful for Summer and if he wasn't able to get to the patient who'd actually hurt her, or visit her, research would have to do. He opened up Google and typed Adrenna hospital into the search bar. As he waited for the old laptop to do its job, he drummed his fingers on his knee.

Almost a million search results popped up. He scrolled through the results until one caught his eye. It was entitled *'The Dark History of Adrenna Hospital'*. Interesting. He checked the name of the website. *Haunted Asylums UK.*

He groaned inwardly. What a crock of rubbish.

He fought the urge to close the laptop and opened up the article. A grey image of the hospital appeared in a separate tab. It was a bird's-eye view and looked vastly different compared to the hospital Swanson had visited that day. It was the same building. The same shape. The same material. Yet somehow it seemed more peaceful, and grass surrounded it, not gravel, while one long driveway stretched from the gates to the impressive front steps.

The haunting turrets at each corner of the square U still stuck out. Raising up from the ground like some sort of monster from the depths or as his Sunday school teacher would have said, something from hell.

He tried to figure out which part of the building he had physically been in during his visit. His finger traced the right-hand side of the building on the screen, the side that had the steel door where they'd entered. A shiver tickled his spine at the memory of the door slamming behind them. The stairs were adjacent and led straight to the first floor. He moved his finger up the screen, roughly to the middle floor of the first turret. He had seen no stairs from there, so how did they get to the very top floor, and what was up there?

He grabbed a small notepad from under the coffee table and removed the pen that he'd shoved into the spine. He made a note:

What's on the top floor?

He scrolled down to read the article and skimmed through the introduction. Adrenna was one of the first purpose-built lunatic asylums in the UK, so it was super old, as he suspected, but it was the history section that caught his eye.

'Dr Brian Stockport was a renowned psychiatrist known for experimental psychosocial treatment with limited use of drugs. He took over Adrenna Hospital during privatisation in the early 1980s. He was well respected in his field and wrote many articles citing successful experiments with using small amounts of diazepam alongside different social treatments.

The history of the Stockport family is a sad one. Two years before taking the hospital over, in 1981, the wife of Dr Stockport was murdered by a burglar who broke into their family home just a couple of weeks before Christmas. She was stabbed to death in their downstairs living room. In 1991, Dr Stockport himself was stabbed by a patient he was trying to help at the hospital, and died. Two weeks earlier, the same patient had murdered a female nurse for the same reason. Both times, the patient stated the devil had told him to do it.

But that isn't the strangest part. Stockport had a son, Jamie Stockport, who took over the hospital after his death. Ten years later, he was also stabbed to death in the same room by a different patient. This patient also said the devil had told him to do it.

Staff and patients often report strange goings on at the hospital. Strange shadows. The devil lurking around corners. Flashes of old Dr Stockport lurking on corners. Is there really a devil who haunts the walls of Adrenna? It seems like it to us.'

Swanson scoffed. Yes. Of course, the devil is happily hanging out in a random hospital in Derbyshire. How can people believe this rubbish? Though Dr Randall had a book on his shelf… Swanson racked his brain. What was it called? *The Devil in Adrenna? The Adrenna Devil?*

He closed his eyes and concentrated on the image there of Dr Randall's office. He remembered looking at the bookshelf as he walked in through the door. Some books about psychiatry and… The Devil of Adrenna! That was it. The kind of stupid story his mother would believe.

Shit. *Mum.*

Should he tell her about the tumour?

With no children or wife, she must be his next of kin. Wouldn't she get his cottage if he died? And his meagre savings?

The thought of calling her filled him with dread. Though her house was only a few streets away, it must have been three years since their last stilted conversation with his stepdad, Ronald, in the background. Listening to every word. Always watching her. She might not even have the same phone number. He had spotted her once since, when he was walking through town with Summer a few weeks ago. She appeared from nowhere on the other side of the cobbles. Their eyes had met, her mouth opened, but quick as a flash Ronald appeared and she turned away. Hurrying off in the other direction.

He wondered if it would be easier to visit and get it over with, rather than call. But as he imagined himself walking down the slabs of her driveway, knocking on the door, and Ronald answering the door… he knew he couldn't face it. She knew where he lived. If she was bothered about how he was she would have visited him before now.

She might even be glad if he was dead. She wouldn't need to feel guilty about not seeing him anymore. Maybe she'd be happier.

Ronald would certainly be glad.

He sat back on the sofa, momentarily putting off his research at the thought of his messed up family. At least if hell was real then his real father would be there to meet him. And if the devil really was at Adrenna, Swanson couldn't wait to ask him all about hell.

He brought up a separate search and googled the book, clicking order before he thought about it too much. One day delivery, nice. There was definitely something off about Adrenna Hospital, and Swanson was going to find out what.

21

Swanson

Swanson opened his heavy eyes, but the darkness was all-encompassing. He couldn't make out a thing. His body ached all over and he stretched his arms with a groan. It must be the middle of the night. Once again, he'd fallen asleep on the sofa.

A rancid, burning smell infiltrated his nostrils. It clogged his throat and made him gag, forcing him to sit up straight on the sofa. What the hell was that? Had he left something in the oven? Meat? A red light in the corner of the darkness caught his half-open eye. He squeezed his eyes and opened them again to focus his blurred vision. The light needed to be turned on. He needed to–

Nausea heaved up from his stomach.

The devil had come for him.

Red eyes were staring at him from a horned and grotesque head. No mouth or body was visible, but Swanson knew what it was.

He tried to stand up, but his body wouldn't move. He was frozen to the spot. Sentenced to sit there and die without a fight.

"You're here for me." He heard his own voice say the words, but his lips didn't move.

The devil didn't reply, but it began to bleed. Blood seeped from the red eyes, just a few tear drops at first. Within seconds the blood ran like a tap, and then a river.

And still Swanson couldn't move.

The blood surrounded him and filled the living room floor. It rose over his feet, then his knees, and he knew he was going to drown in the devil's blood. He closed his eyes and waited for death.

And the heaviness in the room disappeared.

Swanson opened one eye, and the devil had gone. Instead, Dr Randall stood there, surrounded by a pale light. He wore a maniacal grin and pointed a grotesquely long finger at Swanson.

"The devil is here," he said.

"What do you mean?" Swanson again heard his own voice speak, though his lips never moved.

"You already know," Dr Randall said, and disappeared.

As soon as he was gone, daylight filled the room. The heavy feeling and disorientation dissipated. He was free. He stood up and rubbed his face roughly, trying to shake off whatever the hell he had just experienced. His work shirt was soaked through with sweat, as were his hair and beard. His breath came in heavy pants. *What the fuck was that?*

A nightmare? He never even dreamed, never mind had nightmares so vivid. Can you have a nightmare whilst awake? He rubbed his face again. He should have read the side effects on those damn painkillers.

He looked down at his crumpled, damp mess of a suit. It

wasn't unusual for him to fall asleep on the sofa, but he usually managed to at least strip down to his pants first. He stretched and twisted to get his aching body to move and get rid of the pain in his neck. But the memory of Summer made him freeze.

He had to know if she was OK. He rubbed his tired eyes hard and forced them back open to search the living room for his phone. He eventually found it on the floor next to his makeshift sofa bed. Luckily, he'd remembered to put it on charge before falling asleep in a crumpled heap. He had one new text message from Hart sent at 8:00am.

Summer is stable. Go back to sleep.

The clock on his phone informed him it was now 8:30 a.m. He stretched again and yawned loudly. His head was pounding, and his tongue felt like sandpaper. Had he drunk ten bottles of beer last night and forgotten?

He padded through the living room to the kitchen and grabbed a large glass of water, which he downed in one go. He filled it to the brim again and drank another glass full. Flashes of the nightmare kept playing on his mind. What the hell did it mean?

The devil and the blood were fairly obvious. It was clearly something to do with Summer, Adrenna and that damn book he'd ordered. In his mind, images of Summer being attacked had been sneaking in since he heard about what had happened to her. So the blood made sense.

But why on earth would the devil be coming for him?

That was weird as hell.

He needed to speak to Hart. She might have some ideas. After she'd mercilessly taken the piss out of him for letting Adrenna give him nightmares, anyway.

A hot shower washed away the sticky sweat and made him

feel more awake. His brain was working clearly again, his thoughts alive. God knows he needed to feel alive after one of the worst weeks of his life.

He left the bathroom feeling more stable and grabbed the first work suit he saw. The accompanying shirt wasn't ironed, but it would do. He sent a message to Hart to ask her to meet him in the station car park.

He rarely ate breakfast, but his stomach growled. Had he eaten dinner? He couldn't remember. He made a slice of toast and chomped down half of it before jumping into his car.

It had clearly been raining a lot in the night; it soaked the ground through. The sky was still grey, but that was fine. It suited his mood.

It wasn't until he was halfway towards the office on the A52 that he realised what was bothering him. It was now December 2021. The wife died in December 1981. Someone had stabbed the doctor in 1991, and the son in 2001. Each murder was a decade apart, and now someone had stabbed Summer two decades since the last murder. A familiar adrenaline tingled his skin. He punched in Hart's name to the centre console to call her on the hands free system.

"Morning, Krypto," she said in a strangely bright voice.

"What's wrong?" Swanson asked, momentarily thrown by her cheeriness.

"Eh? Nothing. I was being nice. Can't I be nice?" she snapped in her usual, more comforting tone.

"Don't be weird because I have a tumour. It's... weird."

"OK, OK. You're a dick. Better?"

"Much better. Now listen, I was reading up on Adrenna's history and saw all the stuff you mentioned."

"Ooh, the devil stuff and the murders? It's creepy, eh?"

He saw her smug grin in his mind.

"Yeah, and obviously not real."

She tutted, but he continued.

"The doctor who took over the hospital, his wife was killed in 1981. Ten years later, a patient killed the doctor. Ten years after that, a patient stabbed his son. Twenty years later, someone stabs Summer."

"So there's a possibility that the murders are happening every 10 years for whatever reason." Hart cut him off.

"Attempted murder in this case," he said quickly, "and yeah. I mean it's strange and a long shot and probably a coincidence. But I think it's worth looking into at least. Though we're missing 2011."

"Hmm," there was a pause, 'where are you?'

"I'm five minutes away from the station, but I need to stay away from Murray," he said.

"OK, chat to you in the car park in five." A beeping noise filled the car as she hung up.

Swanson raced through the last few streets and reached the car park quicker than he thought. Hart was already there. She was easy to spot in her long red winter coat. Glamorous as ever, despite her sailor's mouth. He pulled up next to her and she jumped into the passenger seat. He drove off, not heading anywhere in particular but wanting to hide away from Murray.

Hart started talking straight away as she pulled off her black leather gloves. "OK. Are you ready for this? I agree with you. And not because you have a tumour. That's purely coincidental. What are you gonna name it, by the way?"

Swanson glanced at her. "Name what?"

"The tumour." She turned to face him.

Swanson was thrown. "Why on earth would I name the

tumour?"

"Because… it's a thing." She waved her hands around as if it would prove her point. "That's what people do. Jeez."

Swanson threw her another look. She was on form today.

She pouted. "Google it and educate yourself rather than looking at me all weird."

"I'm not sure me googling brain tumours is the best idea right now." He pointed out.

She shrugged. "Good point well made."

He needed to change the subject. "So, we need to find out whether someone who thought they were acting on behalf of the devil stabbed Summer."

"OK. I'll call Dr Randall, I guess." Hart pulled her phone out of her handbag. She fiddled around with it and put it to her ear.

"Hi, it's Detective Inspector Hart, I visited yesterday… Good, thank you. Can you put me through to Dr Randall, please?"

She fell silent. Swanson waved a hand to get her attention, but she pushed it away in a huff and ignored him.

"Hello Dr Randall. I need to ask you about the hospital's history, please. I'm aware of what happened to the two Dr Stockport's 10 years apart, and needed to know if there were any other stabbings in the last 20 years that resulted in a death?"

She fell silent for a moment. Swanson glanced at her impatiently. She stuck her middle finger up at him. The supermarket loomed in front of him and he suddenly swerved into the car park. Hart grabbed on to the handle above her passenger side door and shot him an angry look.

"Right, so nothing to do with the doctors?" she said, "OK, thanks for your help."

She put the phone down and sighed as Swanson pulled into

a free space at the back of the car park.

"So?" he asked.

"Nothing to report, really. No other deaths other than a suicide and that was 12 years ago, so doesn't fit with the timeline."

"Fair enough. I knew it was probably a dead horse. Too far-fetched that someone would murder people every ten years. I doubt anyone's even been there that long."

"There is Glenda." Hart turned to look at him with a big grin on her face.

"Glenda?"

"Yes! The old bag receptionist."

Swanson grinned. "Yeah, I imagine she's been there a while!"

"I wouldn't put murder past her. Maybe the doctors didn't sign in one day on her register. A woman's been reported missing, by the way. The day before Summer was hurt. She's a nurse at Derby Psychiatric Unit. She worked on the bank sometimes and covered the odd shift at Adrenna. Bit weird, isn't it?"

Swanson's phone vibrated, and he grabbed it from the centre console. He threw it down and immediately kick started the engine.

"Woah! What's wrong?" Hart asked.

"Forest texted about Summer. She's awake."

22

The Servant

I stared at the text on my phone. The advocate wasn't dead. She hadn't been given to the Devil. The corners of the room blurred into a darkness I couldn't see through. A guttural scream escaped my throat and I let it ring out in the silent room.

Rage coursed through my veins and gave me a new strength. I closed my eyes and time disappeared. But when I opened them a moment later, panting heavily, the room was a whirlwind of mess. The table was turned over, abandoned in the corner of the room. My paperwork from months of research covered the floor like a carpet. The bookshelf was overturned and my precious books were stuck underneath it.

Did I do that? Or did He?

A sharp pain in my hand made me look down. Blood seeped through the cut in my hand. The muscles in my legs and arms ached. And I knew it must have been me who destroyed the room. How could I do that without even realising it? I had to get a grip.

That lying advocate would pay for making me lose myself.

How the hell did she survive when I slashed her right in the throat, as the Devil had asked? A clean but deadly wound with a sharp blade. Well, it should have been deadly. Clearly I'd messed up.

The Devil would not be happy with me. I'd finally found the perfect woman and yet she'd resisted. I had to make it up to Him pronto. She would pay for her insolence. But first, I needed that detective out of our way. Once he was on our side, the rest would be easy.

23

Swanson

Swanson raced out of the car park and spun a left turn, barely beating another car coming from the right which blared its horn. He glanced at the driver in his windscreen mirror and saw him waving his arms about, but ignored him and continued in the direction of the hospital.

"You know, she probably isn't ready to speak to us yet." Hart reminded him. She clung on to the handle above the car door, her knuckles turning white.

"I know. I only want to see if she's OK. She's an important witness. She won't be ready for a full statement."

"Uh, huh. Maybe now you'll finally ask her out." Hart gave him a look.

"Shush," he said, his brow crinkled.

It didn't take long to reach the hospital. Luckily, it wasn't far from the supermarket. And it didn't take that long to reach anywhere in the city centre, really. Swanson sped through Kingsway, his hands sweaty against the steering wheel, and pulled into the colossal car park of the hospital.

Hart pointed to the side of the grass verge. "Pull over here.

Let me park it while you go talk to her. She won't want to see me," she said.

Swanson snorted. "No way. I've seen your parking skills, remember?"

"Do you want to get in there quickly or not?" she huffed.

"Look, there's a space right there." Swanson nodded to a small space on the right-hand side.

"Pfft. You won't get this in there," she said.

"No, *you* wouldn't get this in there," he stopped the car, "if you get out now, I'll pull it in."

Hart jumped out of the car and Swanson forced his brain to focus for one minute as he pulled expertly into the tight space, and squeezed himself out of the car.

"Impressive. I'm surprised you got your massive head out of the door," remarked Hart.

"Me too," he replied.

He marched off in the direction of the entrance whilst Hart hurried behind him. His focus had turned back to Summer. Her face and soft voice filled his head. He entered the hospital and was surprised to find he remembered the way to Summer's room, despite the haziness of his memory when he walked there yesterday.

Hart followed behind him, mostly in silence, much to his relief. Though he probably wouldn't have heard a word she said. His mind was whirring as he waded through the sea of patients, nurses, doctors and porters and everyone else who filled the hospital corridors.

He reached the ward and looked over at the chairs in the corridor. Summer's mother was not there, nor Aaron Walker or her brother. He pressed the bell outside the ward door and waited for a nurse to buzz him inside. Nothing happened.

He buzzed again, and within a few seconds a nurse stalked over to the door. Instead of buzzing them inside, she left the ward and closed the door behind her. She gave them a small smile.

"Hello, can I help?" Her voice was notably light and contrasted with her stern face.

It took Swanson by surprise, and he felt his mouth fall open in shock for a few too many seconds before he closed it again.

"Yes, please. We're here to see Summer Thomas. We heard she's woken up," Hart said when Swanson didn't answer.

"Oh, and are you a relative of Summers?"

Damn. Why hadn't he thought about what to say? Should he say he's a relative?

"I'm... er Detective Inspector Alex Swanson."

"She isn't ready for questions yet," she said.

"Oh no, sorry. I'm not here to ask questions. I want to know if she's OK. I'm also a friend, who happens to be a detective." Christ, he hoped he'd said the right thing.

The nurse considered him for a moment. Then her smile widened, giving her a much friendlier appearance.

"OK. She has a couple of visitors already, so let me tell her you're here, and I'll be right back. You can sit in the chairs there if you like." She pointed at the chairs in the corridor and disappeared back to the ward whilst Swanson stared at her back.

Frustration filled him. His need to see Summer was making him want to lash out. He clenched his fists and stared at the door, focusing on it and willing it to open. Hart stepped back and he glanced around at her. He'd almost forgotten she was there. She'd moved over to the side of the corridor that was lined with chairs.

"I'll wait here. No point in me going in too," she said. "Summer needs friendly faces and rest."

Swanson shrugged and turned back to the ward doors, which he was almost nose to nose with. Had he been that close a moment ago? He took a few steps back and saw the nurse heading towards the door. She was still smiling, at least.

"She's happy to see you. Her other visitors are leaving, so you can come in. You can have a minute or two, then she needs to rest," the nurse explained. He looked down at her name tag which said Sally. She had bruising around her wrist, he assumed from a patient.

He followed her into the ward. Aaron and Summer's mother were inside the door. Her mother didn't look up. If she did she probably wouldn't have recognised him, anyway. But Swanson nodded at Aaron, who had a big grin on his face. He nodded back. Her younger brother followed behind them. He set his mouth in a straight line, and he raised his eyebrow at Swanson as he passed.

Sally led him through the ward to a small private room at the rear. His eyes were drawn straight to the bed, and he smiled his first proper smile in 24 hours. There she was, lying on the bed with her eyes closed. Her skin was even paler than usual, almost grey, and her hair fell limply around her shoulders. A large bandage took up most of the left side of her neck, but she looked peaceful. Serene, even.

"Here's your detective!" Sally said in a loud voice.

Swanson turned to the nurse, ready to shush her. But Summers' eyes flew open, and he forgot about the nurse. Their eyes locked together, and she gave him a small smile.

"I'll leave you to it. Just a couple of minutes, though." Sally wagged one long finger at Swanson before leaving the room.

He stood awkwardly in the middle of the floor, not really knowing what to do now she was in front of him.

"Hey," he said. It was the only word which came to mind.

"Hi," her voice was quieter than usual, and croaked. She waved him closer.

He stepped over to the bed and looked down at her. She pointed behind him, and he turned to see a couple of those plastic chairs he loved so much. Without a word, he reached out to pull one closer; the legs clattering against the tiled floor.

"Oops, sorry," he said as he sat down, "how do you feel?"

She waved a hand at her throat. "Pretty sore, but I'm OK. I need to get home. So hopefully I won't be here long."

"Why the rush? What do you need?" he asked.

"Joshua," she said, her smile disappearing.

"Oh, where is he? Is he OK?"

"At his Dad's. He'll be OK, but he'll also be confused, bless him. He hates being without me. And I hate being without him." She cleared her throat and shifted back into her pillows.

"He'll be fine with his dad, and you need to rest."

The sadness in her eyes made him reach out to her hand and grip it tightly. He looked down, frozen. It was warmer than he expected. Her skin soft. He squeezed her hand gently and put his own back on his lap.

"Don't worry, I'm not here for a statement. But I wondered what you remembered so we can get a head start on investigating what happened?" He got back to a subject he was more comfortable with.

She looked away, her lips pursed. "Erm, it's a bit of a blur. One minute I was talking to Andy and the next someone came at me from the side, hit me in the neck, or at least that's what it felt like, then not much."

That same uncomfortable feeling that had been bugging him since he visited Adrenna Hospital returned.

"Wait, what? Someone came at you from the side?" he asked.

"Yes. Andy was sitting there, but he was pretty out of it. He might tell you more to be honest. But he doesn't talk much. His medication is quite strong."

"Andy is in confinement for attacking you." He instantly regretted saying the words out loud. She snapped her head around to look at him, but winced. She needed to rest, not be bogged down by who did what.

"What?" her face crumpled in confusion, "no. I remember. It definitely wasn't him."

"Are you 100% positive? Don't take this the wrong way, but you're on a lot of painkillers, I presume?"

She let out a soft laugh. "It's not the painkillers. I'm absolutely positive. In fact, it's the only thing I am sure of, because I was looking at him the whole time. He never usually talks at all, like I said. But yesterday he said something to me. He said something about a devil coming for me? But he did not move. I'm sure of it. I think he saw someone behind me, because I heard another voice and blacked out."

"They said something? What was it?"

"Something about the devil. That voice definitely came from behind or on the other side of me. Andy didn't move."

Swanson's nausea returned. Why was the damn devil a constant thing in this?

"Do you know about Adrenna's history?" he asked her.

She looked confused. "Er… no. It's old, I guess. But nothing specific. Why?"

"There's been some weird happenings there. An old Dr went mad, then got stabbed by a patient. His son was stabbed ten years later, in the same room, by a different patient. Both times a nurse was stabbed and killed a week before. And both patients said they were doing it on behalf of the devil."

"What? That's so strange. So you think this patient knew about that and tried to kill me?"

He shrugged. "I don't know what to think yet."

There was a noise as nurse Sally returned through the open door. "Time's up," she said. Her voice was strict again, though she wore a smile.

Swanson glanced at her, and buried the urge to tell her to piss off. He turned back to Summer.

"I'll come back tomorrow?" he said.

"Yeah, if I escape before, I'll let you know." She winked at him.

Swanson reached out to squeeze her hand again, and didn't move at first. But he felt Sally staring at him, and Summer's eyes closed. One short cough from Sally made him shift to his feet. He stalked out of the ward and back to Hart, who was still sitting alone outside.

"How is she?" Hart's face was serious for once.

"She seems OK. A bit sore and groggy from the painkillers," he said, looking back at the ward.

Hart nodded and stood up with a stretch. "Let's get out of here."

He turned back to face her. "She did say something strange, though. She's positive it wasn't Andy who stabbed her."

Hart scrunched up her face. "What? How can she be so sure?"

"She said she was staring at him the whole time. He didn't move."

"Well, I guess that means we're going back to that damn

hospital to see doctor smiley," she replied.

He rubbed at his beard and let out a deep sigh. Adrenna was the last place he wanted to go. But seeing Summer made him even more determined to figure out who had hurt her.

"Fine, but I'm driving."

24

Swanson

Swanson drove them to Adrenna this time, though not as fast as Hart had done. The snaking country roads were wet from earlier rainfall and he wasn't risking his Audi on those twists. They didn't pass many cars on the way. Rush hour was over and most people were now at work or back at home after their school runs.

The high walls surrounding Adrenna loomed into view, and an urge to turn around and drive the other way overcame him. The sight of the prison-like walls made his headache worse and the pit of his stomach filled with dread. There was a god awful feeling about this place, even aside from the fact Summer was stabbed there.

"We should tell Dr Randall to come into the station now," he said, "I'm sick to death of this place."

"Same," Hart muttered, "I agree we should ask him. Get his statement on record properly, seeing as he appears to be mixed up on who hurt who."

Swanson pulled into the car park and chose a space close to the unused front entrance. He raised a hand to the back of his head to dull the ache that had come back with a vengeance. He saw Hart glance at him through the corner of his eye, but she said nothing and clicked her seatbelt. They exited the car and walked around the front corner of the building. He let Hart walk in front of him so he could get a proper look at Adrenna as it towered above him. He wanted to stare it in the eye, get a sense of what was actually causing the sickening feeling in his stomach every time he was here. But the feeling became instantly worse.

Someone was watching them through the top-floor window.

Swanson took a step back to get a better view of the face, but the person disappeared. The curtain fell back into place. Swanson peered at the other windows on the top floor.

"What do you reckon is on that top floor?" he called to Hart, who didn't seem to notice him stop and was now a fair way in front of him.

"I don't know. Storage?" she replied.

He took one last glance at the window, but there was still no face. He jogged over to Hart. "I didn't see any stairs to it anywhere, did you?"

She shook her head and stopped in front of the side entrance. She pressed the buzzer and stood back, waiting for the friendly receptionist to respond. Swanson caught up to her. There was no crackled voice this time though, and the door stayed firmly shut.

Hart buzzed again. They waited, shifting on their feet and kicking gravel. Nothing happened. She put her face up to the camera above the intercom.

"Helloo," she said, waving a hand around above her head as if that would somehow help.

Swanson took a few steps back to the grassy verge and looked again at the top floor.

"Someone was watching us," he told her.

"What?" Hart stepped back to join him on the verge and looked up. She scanned the windows but looked down again and peered at him. "You're seeing things again. Was it an old man with white eyes?"

"No, there was a face in that window. I don't really know what the person looked like. It was a face." He pointed up at the top floor.

"Yeah, a ghostly face with no features... OK. You need to check your meds."

She stepped forward again to the door and pressed the buzzer.

"Third time's a charm," she announced, but she reached into her bag and took out her phone. "I'm going to call Dr Randall. See if he'll come and answer the door."

She raised the phone to her ear as Swanson continued to stare up at the window. He knew he'd seen someone, but who would be on the top floor? Were patients up there or staff?

"No answer." Hart broke him out of his thoughts.

"What the hell is going on at this place?" Swanson gave up on the window and walked forward to stand next to Hart.

She shrugged, one hand on her hip. "Should we wait around, do you think?"

"Let's take a walk around and see if there are any other ways in."

They strolled down the side of the building and rounded a corner to the rear of Adrenna. The wind wasn't so bad here, though Hart still held her coat tightly around her and shivered. Swanson took his woolly hat out of his pocket and threw it at her. She caught it mid-air and pulled it over her head.

Their feet crunching against the gravel was the only noise that echoed out into the silent surroundings. They happened upon another door, barricaded up with wood. No buzzers.

"Where's the secure patient garden?" asked Hart, "you know, like the one in that other psychiatric hospital in the city centre? The one that Lucy disappeared from."

He shrugged and continued around the far corner and down the other side of Adrenna. There were no doors on this side. He kicked the gravel as they reached the car park once again.

"Come on, let's try the buzzer again," Hart said, "one last time before we give up."

"We could really do with finding Summer's brother, Eddie. He was a patient here.' Swanson said as they walked once more to the grey door.

"Yeah, good luck with that," Hart scoffed, "he's long gone."

Once again, no one answered their buzzer, and the pair walked back to the car. Heads down and each lost in their own thoughts.

Swanson snapped his head up suddenly.

"I've got it. We can speak to Aaron. He hasn't worked there for too long, but might be able to help." Adrenaline reignited his brain, and he mentally made a list of questions Aaron might help with.

"Not a bad idea for once," Hart said.

"Thanks, Robin. He might even be inside the hospital as we speak."

"Call him."

His face dropped. "I don't have his number."

"Text Summer and ask her for it. I'm freezing. Let's at least sit in the car."

"You're always bloody freezing," Swanson mumbled. He

couldn't understand how anyone could live their life always being so damn cold.

They walked over to the car and climbed inside. Swanson turned on the engine and put the heater right up, against his better judgement. He texted Summer to ask for Aaron's number.

"I guess we may as well wait here, in case he is inside." Hart sighed as if it was a massive inconvenience.

"She might be sleeping, though. She might not text back for hours, and I'm not waiting here that long. Let's wait five minutes and see what happens. If not, we'll go get a late lunch."

Hart's phone buzzed, and she lifted it to her ear and barked a hello.

"Where? OK. We'll be there soon."

Swanson raised an eyebrow at her. He didn't want to go anywhere yet.

"Someone's found a body. They think it's that nurse. They found her at the site of the devil stone."

25

Summer

The tears threatened to fall, but Summer held them back. She didn't want to scare Joshua off from visiting her.

"I'll come and kiss you better soon, Mummy," Joshua said. His serious blue eyes tugged at her heart.

"I would love that, honey. Maybe tomorrow if you think you'll be OK visiting the hospital?"

He nodded fiercely. "I definitely will be OK. Will you be OK without me now?"

"Aw, honey. I miss you lots, but I'm going to sleep and rest until you get here. I'll be fine."

"And when I come and see you, you'll feel better!" he grinned.

"Absolutely! Have your dinner. I love you lots." She blew him a kiss.

"Love you more!" he shouted.

She laughed. He thought if he said it louder than her, it must be true. She repeatedly blew kisses until he hung up the phone, and plonked it back on the tray in front of her and sat back into the cushions. Her eyes were heavy and thick with sleep, thanks to the morphine. She rarely took so much as paracetamol unless desperate.

The worst part of being stuck in hospital was being away from Joshua. She was lost without her sidekick, and although he was putting a brave face on; she knew he'd struggle to sleep away from her for more than a couple of nights. Though having her own room and being able to sleep uninterrupted was definitely an unexpected bonus of being sliced in the neck.

She closed her eyes and shuffled her head to get more comfortable. Her neck wasn't as painful as she thought it would be with such a wound. A constant dull ache acted as a reminder, though. And having been a side sleeper all her life, getting comfortable on her back was no easy feat.

Despite being in a private room, the staff always left the door wide open and the noise of the ward seeped through. Machines beeped constantly. Conversations were never ending. Then there was the general hustle and bustle of busy nurses, health care assistants and doctors. Luckily, the morphine was strong enough that her mind drifted off even through the noise. Images of Joshua and her cuddling on the sofa played on her mind, with Toy Story or some dinosaur film playing in the background.

Sally's voice brought her back into the hospital room.

"Hey- Oh sorry, I didn't realise you were sleeping! How are you feeling?" She peered at Summer with her head cocked to one side, and gave her a big smile.

Sally was one of the happiest nurses Summer had ever met.

"Hi, Sally. I'm OK. Just tired," she replied, her eyes closing again as though she had no control.

"Oh, good. Are you feeling up to another visitor? Your brother's here."

"Oh sure, let him in." Summer's eyes flew open again, and her heart warmed at the thought of seeing Dylan. He always cheered her up.

"Not for long, though! You need rest," Sally instructed as she swanned back off through the door, returning a few moments later with her brother.

Summer shot up off the pillow and shouted out at the pain in her neck.

"Woah!" Sally put her hands up, "be careful, Summer."

But Summer couldn't speak through the lump in her throat that had appeared.

Standing behind Sally wasn't Dylan, it was Eddie. Summer stared at him. He stared back. His mouth opened, and then closed. He dwarfed the small nurse. Has he always been that tall? He was so clean for a homeless man. His coat and jeans looked brand new.

"Hi, Summer," he said, and looked down towards the floor.

Sally raised her eyebrows at Summer. "Are they happy tears, or does he need to leave?"

Summer shook her head and managed a smile. "No, they're happy tears," she croaked. She waved Eddie over to her bed. He stepped closer but didn't move far. She swallowed hard and lessened the lump in her throat.

"Eddie! Come here," she ordered with a laugh.

He took another couple of steps forward and she reached out and grabbed his hand to drag him in close enough to throw her arm around him awkwardly. He gently placed a hand on her back.

"I don't want to hurt you," he mumbled into her hair.

"I'm so sorry you had to leave, Eddie," she whispered. The lump returned and this time, she couldn't stop the tears from flowing.

Eddie stepped back from her awkward embrace.

"It's me who needs to say sorry," he replied in a quiet voice, looking at the floor again.

After watching for a moment with a small smile on her face, Sally left the room and closed the door behind her.

"Grab a seat. Sit down," Summer gestured towards the stacked pile of chairs.

"OK." Eddie carefully pulled off the top chair from the stack and laid it gently on the floor next to her bed.

"We've been looking for you since Astrid disappeared. Where did you go?" Summer asked. "Are you OK?"

She looked him up and down, taking in his clean cut stubble and freshly washed, short hair. Someone had been looking after him.

"Yes, I've been OK. Better than I've been in years if I'm honest sis. I was in a hostel but got a flat with a friend I met there. I would have told you, but I wasn't sure… and I heard about what happened to you on Facebook and knew I had to see you."

"On Facebook? I didn't realise you were on there?"

"Yeah. I log on sometimes to check up on some people. You included." He smiled at her, but it didn't reach his eyes. "A couple of people have written on your wall saying they were shocked about what happened. I think Dylan put something on. I thought you were dead at first."

His smile disappeared and his face paled. He reached out and took her hand.

"I'm so glad you're OK." He squeezed her hand gently.

"I'd be better if my big brother were around to protect me," she replied. "Maybe we could sort this mess out somehow?"

He took his hand away. "I thought the same thing. You know I didn't bring that gun into the house with Astrid, right? I was trying to get her to admit the truth. I only brought a knife in case she attacked me."

Summer nodded. "I know, Eddie."

"If I speak to the police, they might cart me off to Adrenna, but you and I could at least meet for coffee now and then?" His eyes were wide as he waited for an answer.

But Summer couldn't speak. *Eddie* was right in front of her after all this time. It was as though she were watching the conversation from above.

"Summer? We don't have to meet up if-"

"-No! We can absolutely meet up. I'd love that. And you can meet Joshua."

"Yes, I'd love to meet him.'" He grinned widely and his entire face lit up.

They sat in silence for a moment. It was much quieter with the door closed over, though dulled sounds of machinery and nurses could still be heard. Summer took in the way his hair fell in the same awkward way as Dylan's. And the wrinkles she hadn't noticed amongst the action of their last meeting when he'd saved Astrid. Right before she betrayed him to protect herself.

"If I'm allowed to be a protective big brother now, I need to ask you something important," he suddenly said, breaking her out of her thoughts.

"What is it?" She cocked her head but instantly regretted the movement as pain shot through her neck. Had she pulled a stitch?

"Please don't go back to Adrenna. If I'd have known you were working there, I would have warned you already. It's a hellhole, Summer. You shouldn't go anywhere near it."

Summer kept her face poker-straight. Patients told her many things about the hospitals they were in and it was rarely true. Patients sometimes thought they had been kidnapped, or under a government conspiracy. Summer had to help them call the police. Hospitals were often corrupt to a patient with paranoid schizophrenia and dangerous hallucinations in their head.

If Eddie was paranoid about Adrenna, was Dylan right, and he was still ill? If he was, he'd *have* to stop hiding and get medical help. She squeezed his hand and prepared herself for the worse.

"Why is it so bad?" she asked.

"It's the staff. They're messed up. I used to think it was me, my mental health, my visions. But now I'm doing better, I can distinguish between what was reality and what wasn't."

"I know. The receptionist is awful," she agreed. "But the nurses seem OK?"

He scoffed. "She's more than awful. Glenda Randall is a matriarch. She's the lead psychiatrist's grandma. She was married to the original Dr Stockport before he went mad and stabbed himself."

"Sorry I'm confused. Who stabbed themselves? Is Glenda the receptionist? I thought that was the manager's name."

Eddie nodded. "Some doctor called Stockport in the eighties or nineties, I forget, stabbed himself. Glenda was married to him."

"She was married to the doctor that died? I heard a patient stabbed him." This was giving her a headache.

Eddie shook his head. "He tried to kill a patient as a sacrifice for the devil. He failed, then stabbed himself. And so did his son ten years later. Rumour has it that Glenda killed Dr Stockport's first wife, too. They are doctors who accuse other people of being nuts. But they're the messed up ones, Summer. The rumour is that Adrenna is home to a possessive spirit who calls himself the devil and takes over the doctors. Although now there's only one left."

"There's only one what left?" she asked.

"One Doctor from the family. Doctor Randall. And he's just as nuts as his dad and grandad before him."

26

Swanson

Swanson and Hart arrived at the Hemlock Stone in Stapleford twenty minutes later. Summer had replied with Aaron's number, so Swanson sent him a text to ask if he was at work. The two-hundred-million-year-old sandstone tower stood almost thirty feet tall, the top half black and the bottom half red. Otherwise known as the devil's stone because of the myth that he had thrown it from the nearby town of Castleton when the ringing of church bells across the town annoyed him.

"The Stone Cross is in Stapleford," Swanson muttered as they sludged across a muddy field.

"What are you muttering about?" Hart threw him an unimpressed look.

"The oldest Christian monument in the midlands is over there." He pointed toward St Helen's Church, which lay on the other side of the small town.

"Full of useful information you, aren't you?" She pulled one stuck boot out of a particularly muddy piece of grass, staring down at it with distaste.

"Yep. More useful than ghost stories."

She jabbed him in the side and stumbled off the grass, onto the path that led towards the stone. Someone had already erected a large white tent and various forensic specialists donning white gear swanned around the area.

"Do you know anything about this nurse?" Swanson called after her as he reached the path. He traipsed his shoe along the path to get rid of the muddy chunks.

She slowed her pace and turned around to face him. "Er, not much more than what I said. I saw the press briefing. Didn't you see it?"

"I've been preoccupied." He pointed to his head.

"Well, her name was Sharon Vaughan. She was fairly young, about our age, maybe early thirties. And not married, because her boyfriend called her in as missing. No kids, I don't think. Her primary job was at Derby Psychiatric Hospital, but she took the odd shift at Adrenna as a bank nurse when they were short staffed. She disappeared early Wednesday morning after finishing a night shift."

"The day before Summer got stabbed," Swanson mused as they reached the crime scene boundary.

A uniformed officer checked their ID's and allowed them to pass through. Swanson spotted a familiar face a few feet away. Detective Inspector Ryan Thomas. An ex-colleague from Nottinghamshire Police and a useful person to have on your side. He raised a hand to Thomas in acknowledgement, who grinned and walked over to meet them.

"Hi, stranger. What's the great Alex Swanson doing back here in Nottingham?" He laughed, and nodded to Hart, who was around the same height as him. She gave him a small nod in return. "You haven't moved back over to the dark side, have you?"

"Not yet, mate." Swanson grinned. "But we do think you have one of our missing persons back there."

"Yeah, I heard someone from Derby would come over. Didn't hear your name mentioned though."

"It's not exactly our case, but we are working on something else which involves… well, a devil."

"Oh, I see. That's a pretty strong connection. Well, we can't get any closer at the minute."

"Can you tell us about the note?" Hart asked.

Thomas looked around to make sure nobody else could hear, then repeated in a low voice, "The dogs always bark, and the violets die a death, when the devil brings the dark, and when he gets inside my head."

Hart whistled. "Well, that's creepy as hell."

Thomas let out a short laugh. "You could say that."

"And the body?" Swanson asked.

"The body was left naked and in no particular position. Someone has dumped it as it lies. There's bruising and a big wound on the neck so it looks like a slit throat. There's also bruising to both wrists, as if they tied or cuffed her to something. Yet they'd piled the clothes neatly next to the body. Forensics are all over it at the minute."

"So, the body was just dumped? But they'd taken care to neatly fold the clothes?" Hart asked.

Thomas nodded. "That's what it looks like. I assume we'll be sending over the images and forensics to your teams soon."

Swanson nodded. "Thanks, Thomas."

"This reminds me a bit of that case we worked on years back, my first murder. Do you remember? A naked woman in a park. The suspect punched you in the face." Thomas snorted.

"Yes, busted my lip." Swanson grinned at the memory.

"Turned out not to be him. We never caught that guy. Might be worth looking into it."

Swanson stepped away as Thomas walked off and motioned for Hart to follow him.

"So, we have someone talking about the devil before stabbing Summer. A woman, a nurse who sometimes works at Adrenna, murdered outside of the hospital. Her body laid out similarly to a murder from years ago. A history of nurses being murdered, right before a doctor gets murdered. It looks like history is repeating itself alright."

"It must all be linked somehow. What happened to the previous body?" Hart furrowed her brow.

"Hard to remember now. It was about ten years ago. But she was naked in a park with her clothes folded neatly. She was a young student, not a nurse, but we definitely need to look into it. I think I'll talk to Summer again. She might remember more as she recovers."

"Ten years ago? Our missing 2011 murder? I think we need to talk to Dr Randall, too. He might know more about the history of the hospital and he might be in danger as the doctor. Don't some patients get leave that would enable them to leave the hospital alone?"

"Yes, sometimes. It's quite hard to get it approved, though."

"Not impossible that they could have attacked the nurse on leave."

"No, just unlikely. Still worth crossing off the list."

Swanson thought hard as they crossed the slimy field back to his car. Whoever had murdered Sharon Vaughan sounded like they were obsessed with the devil. Before all doctor murders, a nurse was stabbed. And now a nurse, followed by an advocate, had been stabbed again.

"So Summer being stabbed could be a coincidence, and nothing to do with this devil business. But it's unlikely because she heard someone say something about the devil right before she was stabbed. Or, scenario 2, they were not happy with only killing this nurse, and wanted another woman for some reason." Swanson thought aloud.

"Like what?" Hart asked.

"Maybe it was a mistake with the nurse. She wasn't right, so he stabbed Summer instead."

Hart treaded carefully through the sodden grass as they left the path, trying to miss the muddiest parts. "But Andy is locked away. He couldn't have killed the nurse."

"But Summer said it wasn't Andy who hurt her. We need to know what patients were on that ward, and if any are allowed unsupervised leave. Or if any have any kind of obsession or association with the devil."

Hart finally looked up at him as they reached the car park. "What if it wasn't a patient?"

"As in a member of staff? Don't tell me you're blaming Glenda." Swanson raised an eyebrow as he lifted the boot of his car. "Do not get in my car yet."

Hart snorted. "Wouldn't put it past her. And why am I not allowed in your car?"

"Here." He handed her two empty carrier bags.

"Erm. Thanks?" She said as she took them from him.

"They're for the floor. I don't want mud in the car."

She muttered something under her breath as she walked over to the passenger door, bags in hand.

"You're right, though," Swanson called over the top of the car as he pulled off his loafers and replaced them with the clean trainers in his boot. "We need the names of the staff on the ward and the patients. Whoever did this might have attempted two murders in as many days. We need to prevent a third."

He put his muddy shoes into a third empty carrier bag and threw them into the boot. No doubt he would forget they were there and be looking for them in the morning.

"Well, if this person knows Summer is alive, they might try to get to her," Hart called to him from the front seat.

Shit. She was right. Summer needed some sort of protection on the ward. The thought of her getting hurt again made him feel nauseous. His seat groaned as he jumped into the driver's side, when another thought hit him.

"Or, if they think Summer *is* dead, they might go after the doctor next if history is to be repeated," he said as he pulled his seatbelt across.

"So if it's the same pattern, a doctor's going to get stabbed soon. With the previous doctors, the nurses were stabbed two weeks prior."

"So if that is what's happening, we've hopefully got some time. But I think we need to at least warn Dr Randall that he could be in danger." Swanson reversed out of the park and pulled out onto Coventry Lane.

"I don't know if he is, but I find it strange that he didn't mention any of the history to us," Hart mused.

"Maybe he didn't know?" Swanson said, hazarding a guess, but it was a weak explanation. How could Dr Randall not know? He thought back to their visit to his office. He had been super friendly. His office was typical of a messy professor. He remembered seeing something there, though.

"The damn book!" he said aloud.

"You know what a book is?" Hart put her hand to her mouth

and laughed.

"Dr Randall had a book. It was called The Devil of Adrenna or something like that. I ordered a copy yesterday. I conked out after and forgot all about it to be honest. Tell you what, I'll drop you off at the station so you can get your car and talk to Murray about protection for Summer. And I'll call you once I've gotten home if the book has arrived.'

"Fine, but one way or another we are going to end up back at Adrenna, aren't we?"

Swanson didn't answer, though he knew she was right. That damn hospital would be the death of him. As long as it wasn't the death of Summer, he could live with that.

27

Swanson

Swanson carefully weaved the Audi through the labyrinth of inner city streets. Hart was trying to call Dr Randall for the second time after her first attempt went ignored. He glanced over at her and saw her expression set in a stubborn grimace.

"He's not going to answer now if he didn't answer five minutes-."

Hart suddenly jumped forward in her seat and waved a hand in his direction to shush him.

"Yes, hello Dr Randall. It's Detective Inspector Hart here. I'm sorry to bother you again, but we could do with asking you a few more questions. Can you come down to the station, please?"

Swanson heard the high-pitched voice of Randall, though he couldn't make out the words. He shuddered at the noise.

"Yes, that would be OK. Thank you, Dr Randall." Hart put the phone back into her bag.

"He said he will come down later today as long as nothing happens on the wards. He seemed quite happy to speak to us again."

"He's always happy, seemingly. Maybe I should sneak into the back without Murray seeing so I can chat to him with you."

"Yeah. You're great at sneaking. No one ever notices you when you walk into a room." She turned to him and smiled sweetly.

Swanson tutted. He couldn't deny she was right, though. "Fine. I'll go home. Call me as soon as he's gone," he replied as he pulled into the station car park.

He left the engine running as Hart jumped out. She turned to him before closing her door and gave him another one of her out of character looks.

"Listen, make sure you call me later. Or at least text, OK?"

"Jesus, Hart. Stop fussing. I appreciate it but I'm honestly fine." Swanson furrowed his brow and stared straight ahead out of the windscreen.

"Think if it was the other way round, how would you react? You'd want to know I was OK, right? So let me know. See you later." She waved, then slammed the car door. He watched her small frame stalk off to the entrance of the police station. She was right again, he supposed. It wouldn't be hard to send her a two second text later on.

He turned out of the station and headed toward his cottage. He circled Pentagon Island, intending to dive off onto the A52 towards home, yet something pulled him further on to take the exit back into the city. An urge to see Summer.

He considered what Thomas had said about the previous case in Grosvenor Park. They'd interviewed a weedy young student at the time, though his name escaped Swanson's tired brain. When Swanson pushed questions about his sex life, he'd gotten mad and punched Swanson in the face. His alibi had been watertight in the end, anyway. Swanson moved to Derbyshire, and they didn't find the killer.

He called Hart on the hands free and waited for her to answer. As usual, it didn't take her long.

"Hey, look can you look into that murder Thomas mentioned? It was at Grosvenor Park. I wanted to know the name of the suspects."

"OK. I'll look."

He hung up and found himself in Derby Hospital's car park a few minutes later, swearing once again at the tightness of the spaces. At least at Adrenna there was no one else around to park right next to you. Though there was pinging gravel to worry about instead.

He tried to forget about his car as he walked into the hospital and back to the lift to get to Summer's floor. His phone buzzed, and he tugged it out of his suit trouser pocket. He felt a little hole in the pocket and cursed. They were £45 from a well-known high street brand, and he'd expected them to last longer at that price. He looked at his phone and saw a missed call and a new text message. The hospital had left him a voicemail.

He stood outside Summer's ward and dialled voicemail to listen. His heart thumped in his chest as he waited for the message to begin.

'Hi, Alex. It's Dr Tiffin here. We don't have a date yet for your biopsy, but should have one by tomorrow. I need you to be ready to come in. I also wanted to remind you to take the medication I gave to you yesterday. It's difficult to admit that we're ill sometimes, but it's very important that you take it and don't allow yourself to suffer. I'll call again tomorrow to check in.'

Swanson let out a slow, controlled breath. No date yet. OK.

He forced his mind to change to Summer, and buzzed the bell to be let into her ward. He saw the same nurse as before walking over to the door. What was her name? Sam? Sarah? She smiled and buzzed him in.

"Hello, Mr Swanson, wasn't it?" she said as he pushed open the door.

"Yes, hi…" he racked his brain, "Sally. How is Summer?"

"She's doing well. This way."

Sally led him through the busy ward to Summer's room and poked her head in to tell Summer he had arrived. He had a moment of panic. He really should have texted her first to let her know he was on his way. A wave of relief ran through him as he heard Summer tell her to let him in.

He stepped inside the room. To his surprise, Summer was sitting up on the bed. Her sallow skin made her look tired, but she looked much happier than on his last visit. He pulled out one chair and placed it next to her bed.

"How are you feeling?" he asked.

"I'm OK. It doesn't hurt as much as you'd think, actually," she said.

"Or you're super tough?" he smiled.

"Yeah, there's that too, obviously." She winked at him and laughed.

"Listen. There's been some developments." He stopped. How on earth was he going to word it without scaring her?

"OK. Go on?"

"Well, if you said it wasn't Andy who did this, we need to find out who it was. And that means we need to put an officer near you for a night or two to ensure whoever it was doesn't come back."

'So, do you think he might come after me again?' Her eyes

widened.

He was silent for a moment, and caught sight of her pale hand in front of him. He reached out before he considered what he was doing and wrapped his hand around hers.

"I will not let that happen, Summer." He squeezed her hand. "Hart is with Murray right now asking for someone to sit with you. Or at least outside the ward."

Her eyes flickered downward to their entwined hands. She pushed her thumb out from under his hand and wrapped it around his palm.

"I have something to tell you." She didn't look up. "Eddie… left me a message. He said not to go back to Adrenna. It's dangerous. He said the receptionist is the wife of the old doctor who took it over in the 80s, and she killed his first wife. He also said that the doctor went mad and tried to kill a patient, and stabbed himself when he failed. And ten years later, his son did the same thing."

Swanson tensed and pulled his hand away from her, leaning back in his chair. "That's not what I read," he frowned, "and how did Eddie get a message to you?"

"He said some patients believe the devil himself lives there, and he's in the walls. Inescapable. If he chooses you then you have to do what he says." She shuddered. "I always hated going there."

"Maybe he's right. It isn't a safe place to work."

"You're the third person to say that in as many days." She turned away and shuffled back into the pillows.

"Well, you are in a hospital bed," he pointed out.

She laughed softly. "Yes, I can't argue with that, can I?"

"Did Eddie say anything else in this message that you're refusing to tell me how he delivered?" He wondered if Eddie had the balls to come and visit Summer in the hospital. Surely not?

"He said Glenda, the receptionist, is Dr Randall's gran. She was married to the original doctor, and Randall was his grandson, but changed his name somehow. Or just lies about his name. He wasn't really sure."

"Dr Brian Stockport? Dr Randall is his grandson? That nasty receptionist is his gran?"

Summer nodded, but winced and put her hand to her neck.

"You OK?" Swanson asked, though his brain was whirring. Little jigsaw pieces of information flew around his thoughts in a whirlwind.

"I'm fine." She put her hand down and rearranged her head on the pillows once more.

He gritted his teeth and forced his face to stay neutral to not alert Summer. He stood up and gave her hand one last squeeze before he walked away. "I'll let you get some rest. If you remember anything else, call me. No matter what time, OK?"

"Oh, I did remember something else actually," she called out as he was halfway towards the door.

He turned to face her.

She continued. "I meant to text you but I forgot. It's the morphine making me dozy. The devil brings the dark."

"Sorry, what?"

"The devil brings the dark. I think that's the last thing I heard. The muttering I mentioned about the devil? The devil brings the dark and gets inside my head."

Swanson didn't respond, didn't move.

"Are you OK?" Summer asked.

"Er, yes. Sorry. That's a weird thing to say, isn't it? Look, I need to go but I'll catch up with you soon. Let me know if you remember anything else, or need anything. An officer should sit outside the ward soon."

He walked off without waiting for a response. The familiar adrenaline of getting closer to the culprit was rushing over him. This was their proof that whoever was involved with the murder of Sharon Vaughan was also involved with stabbing Summer. Now, he had to find out who on that ward was obsessed with the devil. And if Dr Randall was the grandson of Brian Stockport, he must be intertwined with the story somehow. He might be the next one to die.

28

Swanson

Dusk fell as Swanson crawled through the tail end of the rush hour on the A52. The clock on his dashboard ticked past 6pm. Aaron hadn't texted back about whether he was in Adrenna, but it didn't matter now.

Randall had agreed to meet Hart in the station for a chat at 6:30pm. Swanson texted her a list of questions and told her about Summer's update. Now it was a waiting game. So he headed four miles east to the sleepy town of Ockbrook, where his cottage lay close to the top of the hill. It was half-hidden by the nave roof of the stunning Moravian Church building. Ockbrook was home to one of very few Moravian settlements in the UK, something Swanson tried not to think about since his last conversation with his very religious, and estranged, mother. She wasn't part of the settlement, but any church acted as a reminder.

He pulled into the driveway and stretched as he got out of the Audi. His eyes felt heavy already, such was the stress of the week so far. The air was still thick with the earthy smell of petrichor.

But the hair on the back of Swanson's neck raised despite the musty air, and he peered at the narrow street behind him, unable to shake a feeling that eyes were on him from somewhere.

There were no street lamps near his cottage on Bay Lane, and the tall church blocked out what little was left of the natural light. He watched for a moment, but nothing appeared.

He walked over to the front door, and there, on the doorstep, was a brown package. He picked it up, relieved it was heavy enough to be a book.

"The Devil of Adrenna," he muttered, "I'll be getting to know you soon."

He took one last look behind him before entering the cottage. The streets were still other than an overly fluffy cat sitting on the opposite side of the road. It stopped licking its front paw and peered at Swanson with untrusting eyes. He glared back for a moment, then disappeared inside the cottage, slamming the door behind him.

He kicked off his shoes as soon as he got inside, leaving them by the bottom of the open staircase in front of the doorway. The cottage was too small for a hallway. It was more of a 'hallsquare'. He walked through the wonky lounge to the kitchen, which was just as crooked, and tore the strip off the brown package from the doorstep. A small book fell out when he turned the package upside down.

The Devil of Adrenna was only an inch thick. He flicked it open and breathed in the new book smell. It had been a long time since he'd read a book thanks to work and general adult duties, but as a child that woody scent had been his favourite smell

He flicked through the pages and took in the detailed pictures of Adrenna in its heyday. The writing was fairly large, it wouldn't take too long for him to skim through. He'd pored through much bigger books in a couple of days as a teenager. He flicked through the introduction first, which went into the history of the development of the hospital.

From the late 1960s, the various asylums in the UK were closed down and emptied - of the living, at least.

Swanson rolled his eyes, but kept flicking through. He read more carefully as he got to the next chapter.

There are few buildings which remain and are used as modern day psychiatric hospitals, but Adrenna is one that lives to tell the tale. It doesn't take much to realise the rumours must be true. One step into the gardens of this beautiful building and you know that something is watching you.

The face in the window of the top floor at Adrenna came to Swanson. He shuddered, despite his belief that ghosts weren't real. He couldn't disagree that the feeling of being watched stayed with him. He looked up at the kitchen window. The plain green curtains were wide open, though all he saw in the window was his reflection. Anyone could stare right at him and he wouldn't have a clue. He walked over to the window and closed them tight, before double checking he'd locked the back door. Then he leant back on the kitchen counter and continued to read.

The book moved on to a quick overview of the victims of the Adrenna stabbings. At the last paragraph, he froze. He flicked his eyes back to the start of the line to re-read, but there it was in black and white.

This book will go into more detail about each victim, but one thing was the same for each one. The calling card of the devil himself. A

poem, left by those who he has haunted:
　'The dogs always bark,
　And the violets die a death,
　When the devil brings the dark,
　And when he gets inside my head.'

29

Swanson

Swanson sent a quick text to Hart to remind her to call him about Dr Randall as soon as their interview was complete and crossed the cottage to the living room. He closed the curtains, which were the same plain green as the kitchen, and flicked on the TV for some background noise. Celebrity Catchphrase played out, though he only recognised one contestant, an ex-soap star. The laptop clanged off the side of the coffee table as he pulled it out from the underneath storage section, and he sunk into the end seat of his two-seater sofa, ignoring the creak it gave under his weight.

He tapped his leg as he waited for Google to load. The laptop always took a minute or two to get going. He watched the catchphrase contestants try to guess what the screen was showing. A stunt bike rider flew up and down a skate ramp, before taking off his helmet to reveal a winking devil. '*Daredevil*' shouted one contestant. Even watching random TV programs he couldn't get away from the devil.

He tore his eyes away and focused on his laptop. He typed in the words of the devil's poem and waited for the results to pop up. But a faint knocking sound made his head shoot up again.

Was that an actual knock at *his* door?

If there was one thing he didn't get, ever, it was unannounced visitors. He stared at the door. It didn't move. Had he expected it to?

It must be bloody charity door knockers. They would go away if he ignored it. There was no way he was dealing with salespeople right now. He looked back at the laptop and tried to focus on the random results that had popped up. Nothing seemed to match.

Knock. Knock. Knock.

Swanson threw the laptop to his side and stood up. He stared at the door for a moment angrily, building up to answer it and make the caller go away. He stalked over and yanked it open, ready to let loose at a cold seller who had ignored his signs.

A stocky woman in her fifties stood there, with the same fine hair and light eyes as him. Eyes that were peering nervously up at him. He sucked in a breath, and his body went rigid.

Was he dreaming again?

"Hi, Alex," she said, her voice soft.

"Mum?" His voice came out much higher than usual.

"Hi," she said again. She looked down at the ground and tucked a stray hair behind her ear. "I'm sorry for randomly turning up."

He said nothing at first. He had an urge to reach out and touch her, to make sure she was real. But he didn't want her to think he was losing the plot. Even though he might be, with old blind men following him around. She returned her gaze to him.

"Is something wrong? Are you OK?" Swanson racked his

brain for any reason his mother would turn up unannounced at his doorstep after they'd barely spoken in forever. "Is Aunt Barb OK?"

She nodded and tucked a stray piece of flyaway hair behind her ear. "Yes, yes. Everyone is fine. But... are you OK?"

"Yes, of course." His face crumpled in confusion. "Why wouldn't I be?"

"I don't know. I felt a need to check." She fell silent.

It didn't happen often, but his mind went blank. He could interrogate all the 'no comment' givers all day long, yet here he was lost for words with his own mother. She said nothing either. He cursed himself. She peered up at him, and he cleared his throat. Her perfume seeped through. He hadn't smelt that in three years.

"Want to come in?" he asked, suddenly wanting to keep the smell. To hear her laugh. Maybe even to tell her about the tumour.

"Oh no, you don't need to invite me in." She waved a hand.

He hesitated, opened his mouth, then closed it again. He studied the woman in front of him. Since their last argument, he'd thought about her a lot. More wrinkles lined her face now. Her hands looked fragile as she clasped them together. If anything were to happen to her...

"No. It's OK. Come in, if you want to?" he said.

She peeked behind him shyly. "Do you live alone? I actually thought I saw you a few weeks ago... with a woman? I didn't want to intrude."

His cheeks flushed with warmth. "Yes, but I'm sure Aunt Barb keeps you updated on that front."

She laughed softly. He felt a lump in his throat. It had been too long since he'd heard her laugh.

"Actually Mum–"

"Well I–"

Their awkward laughter rang out into the empty street, and the lump in his throat disappeared. It felt good to laugh with her again.

"You go," Swanson said.

"I, well, I was about to head off. I wrote my address down though, in case you ever wanted to pop by." She handed him a piece of scrap paper.

He eyed her warily as he took the piece of paper with her address neatly written in black ink. Her handwriting had always been super neat. Not like his own, which was so bad he could barely read it back himself.

"I've left Ronald so, you know, it would be nice to see you. I know you'll need time to think about it, so I'm going to go, and give you that time." She hesitated, but turned around and stepped away from the front door.

Swanson stared at the piece of paper she had given him, unable to look back up at her. Halfway down the drive, she called out, "I love you." and continued on her way.

He didn't move from the open doorway as she walked away. He watched her leave his drive and disappear down the street. Part of him wanted to run after her, but she was right. He needed some more time. He needed to think about it and have a plan, so it wasn't too awkward. And he had to decide if he was going to tell her about the tumour. Once she'd disappeared out of view, he stepped back inside and closed the door softly behind him. He leant against it, worried he'd made the wrong decision. *Would she even want him to run after her?*

His phone buzzed from somewhere in the living room and broke his trail of thought. He looked up and saw it flashing on the sofa next to the laptop. He crossed the room in a trancelike state, his sense of urgency momentarily lost thanks to his mother's impromptu visit.

And he'd thought having a tumour would be his shock of the week. *Pfft.*

Though if he was going to be sick, having his mother around certainly wouldn't be a bad thing. After all, he might not be around much longer to make things up with her. And if he really was at risk of dying soon he wanted to make up with his mother. He should call Aunt Barb. She was great for talking things through.

Time seemed elongated as he walked to the sofa, as if an hour had passed when it had only been sixty seconds. He grabbed the phone. It was from Hart.

'Hey, no officer for Summer yet. Murray is looking into who to assign. Randall hasn't shown yet, going to call him now. Suspect from the Grosvenor Park body in 2011 was called Billy Logan.'

No officer for Summer and Randall was missing? Panic fluttered through Swanson like a swarm of butterflies. He grabbed his car keys and rammed his feet back into his trainers. As he left the house, he locked the door behind him and called Summer. He reached the Audi, and pressed the button to unlock the door.

The swishing sound of the car unlocking was the last thing he heard before everything went black.

30

The Servant

Getting Alex Swanson back to Adrenna wasn't as hard as I thought it would be. Not with the help of the Devil. I couldn't stop grinning. He would be a prize for the Devil and he'd be Summer's protector. I'd be honoured forever by His side.

I studied him through the darkness. The light wasn't good down here, only one bulb worked and that was in the far corner. He slumped against the wall, his eyes still closed. I'd made sure I locked his cuffs tight. They were unbreakable, made for keeping severely disturbed people shackled up. He wouldn't be going anywhere.

Not until I knew what the advocate had told him about the attack. Then he would go to see the Devil.

It didn't take long for him to stir and stretch. He groaned and the rattling of metal rang out, echoing through the cellar. I stepped back, suddenly unsure of how far the metal chains stretched. His eyes flicked open, but closed again.

"Hello." I tried to sound concerned, but couldn't prevent a hint of glee entering my voice.

His eyes flickered open again, and he tried to move an arm. The chain rattled and stopped short, making a loud clanging noise. His eyes suddenly opened wide and peered around his surroundings. And finally, he spotted me.

"Hello, Alex Swanson," I tried again. I could be patient. We had all night.

"Who is that?" his voice was dry and croaked.

"Dr Randall," I said. He needed some water. I picked up the bottle I'd left on the floor and opened it up, stepping forward. "Here."

I held the open bottle to his lips. He looked up at me and shook his head, his squinted eyes flashing with rage.

" Maybe later," I said, moving back towards the door and giving him some space to acclimatise to his surroundings. He looked all around the room and took heavy breaths, eventually his eyes settled back on me. The rage was gone, and his breathing slowed.

"Why am I tied up?" he asked.

"Well, because you're bigger than me, and I didn't think you'd listen to me otherwise. We need to talk. I have a fantastic proposition for you." I would have thought that was obvious.

"I agree we need to talk. That's why my colleague Rebecca Hart asked you to come and see us at the station. I won't hurt you."

He lied to me. I snorted and shook my head. "Of course you will. Why wouldn't you?"

"Why would I?" He feigned confusion, but I *knew* he realised what was going to happen. He must have some sort of idea, at least.

"Because I'm going to kill you," I said simply.

He didn't react at all to my words. He continued to stare

at me, his neutral expression giving nothing away. It was impressive.

"What did you do to me?" he asked.

"Ah. Well, sometimes we have to help patients to sleep quickly if they need to settle down. I used an injection of Halmodol to pop you off to sleep so we could get you into the van."

"Well, I feel like shit," he groaned.

"Yes, it can do that to you. I apologise. But that won't matter for long. Water will help." I pointed to the bottle, which still lay full at my feet.

"Wait." His head snapped up. "You said *'we'*?"

I said nothing. Did I say *we* or was he trying to trick me?

"Did you mean the devil?" he asked.

"The Devil?" I asked slowly, unsure of what he already knew. How would he know about my connection to Him?

"Has the Devil spoken to you?" I asked. "Or was it her?"

"Who?"

"That stupid advocate who was supposed to die. Summer." I spat her name out, still furious with her. "Your friend, so I've heard."

I watched his reaction. His face turned a shade of red, fists closed over. Yet his face was still neutral. "It was you who hurt her, wasn't it?" he asked.

I chuckled. "No, of course not. It was Him. And only to give her a better life, Alex Swanson. Which is why I want to talk to you. "

"Who is *him*?"

"The Devil. He's been with my family for thirty years and now I'm honoured to be a part of our history."

"I know about the devil and your family."

I thought I'd misheard him at first, but I didn't. He knew. Had I been tricked? How could he possibly know?

"What do you think you know?" I asked.

"I heard about what happened. That your grandad and dad stabbed themselves. They thought the devil was after them."

I laughed. "Is that what you heard? That's not true. You've been reading too many things on the internet."

He shifted on the ground onto his knees. I took a step back, wary of getting too close even if he had chains on.

"Don't step back, I just have a leg ache. OK? What happened? Tell me the full story."

I eyed him with suspicion. I'd told no one the full truth before. It might be good to share the story. Surely He wouldn't mind because Swanson was going to meet him soon, anyway.

"You're going to kill me, anyway. You may as well tell me the truth."

"OK. I'll tell you the truth. But will you tell me what the advocate said about me? I need to know to protect us."

"Of course." he nodded as if it was the most simple conversation in the world.

I suppose I had no choice but to trust him. And even if he didn't hold up his end of the bargain, there were other ways to get the truth out of people, and the Devil knew all about them.

31

Swanson

Swanson fought through the thumping pain at the base of his neck. He struggled to pick out coherent thoughts through the fog in his brain. He gently leant forward to pull on the chains around his arms. They felt weak, old. And as he leant, he felt them weakening further. He just had to keep Randall talking.

"OK. I'll tell you," Dr Randall said, nodding his head as if pleased with his decision.

He looked eerie in the warm glow of one yellow bulb glowing somewhere behind him in the cellar. At least, Swanson assumed it was a cellar. Darkness hid Randall's left side, but his right was lit up with the glow. With his floppy hair, large glasses and white doctor's coat, he looked more like a mad scientist than a psychiatrist.

"Thank you." Swanson forced the words out in a calm and steady voice, though his tongue was like sandpaper. Bits of previous training sessions floated around in his mind. *Create a relationship. Get them talking. Humanise yourself.* He kept glancing at the bottle of water. It looked untampered with. He was tempted to risk it.

"When I was a boy, I thought the devil was talking to me in my dreams. I didn't like it. I didn't appreciate how special it was at the time. But my dad knew. He told me how special it was. It was him that made me listen to these dreams. Though Grandma tried to stop it."

Swanson swallowed. This guy was more messed up than he'd realised. Randall looked down at the floor as he spoke, and Swanson took a chance to peer past him. There was no way he had dragged him here alone. Someone else must be close by.

"Glenda is your grandma, right? What did the devil tell you to do?"

Randall looked back up, and Swanson forced himself to focus on him.

"Small things at first. Steal something from the local shop. Trip someone over at school. It was all to test my loyalty to him, you see. That's what Dad said."

A shiver ran through Swanson. The air was thick with damp, but his shiver had nothing to do with being cold. "Did you ever disobey?" he asked.

"Yes. The day my dad was stabbed to death." Randall looked down again. His eyes were watering as he reminisced.

"So, someone else stabbed your dad? He didn't stab himself?"

"What? Of course he didn't stab himself," Dr Randall spat, his eyes flashing. Swanson said nothing. "The Devil took control of my grandma, and *she* stabbed him."

So Glenda was a murderer, after all. Hart would be pleased. It took him a moment to realise he was laughing out loud.

"Why are you laughing?" Dr Randall demanded. "Do you not believe me?"

Swanson swallowed hard and forced the laughter back. "I believe you completely," he said as sincerely as he could. "I think the drugs you gave me are making me act funny."

Dr Randall relaxed. "Oh. Yes, they will make you more calm. Do you feel OK? I know about the tumour."

"What tumour?" It was Swanson's turn to tense up. How on earth could Randall know about that? Only he and Hart knew. "Do you have access to my medical records?"

A noise at the end of the corridor made them both snap around. Swanson couldn't see a thing from where he was shackled to the wall.

Randall grinned. "He's here."

A shadow appeared in the light of the weak bulb, then disappeared quick as a flash.

"The dogs always bark, and the violets die a death, when the devil brings the dark, and when he gets inside my head." Randall lifted his arms into the air, eyes closed tight.

Swanson heard quick footsteps heading towards them. His heart raced and he pulled again at the shackles. Maybe his Sunday school teacher was right, and he really was going to see the devil.

32

The Servant

He was coming. I squeezed my eyes shut tight as I waited for the familiar icy breeze to wash over me. He would be happy with me today. And I couldn't wait to show Swanson how special he was.

"To be a messenger of the Devil is a wonderful honour to bestow." I told him.

"Why would the devil want me?" he asked. I sensed the fear in his voice.

"You're everything he needs! Vigilant, alert, serious. You need to protect her when he's busy." I felt the Devil getting closer. His presence was engulfing.

"Who am I supposed to protect? Dr Randall, please listen to me. I think we need to talk some more."

"Your advocate, of course. Summer." I smelt the Devil now. His stench was overpowering.

"How can I protect her if I'm dead? You're not making sense."

"She won't be alive for long. She is perfect for Him. Don't you see?"

"And why would she need a protector if she's with the devil?

This doesn't make any sense to me?"

"You're the protector for when He isn't around. She is for Him, the Devil himself. Do you feel weak yet?"

"Why would I feel weak?" His voice was high pitched now.

I opened my eyes to take him in one last time. His face was ashen, and sweat dripped down his forehead. He looked behind me and his eyes widened.

I grinned. He was here. I turned to wait for Him. I took the knife out of my pocket and held it in the air.

Footsteps sounded in every direction of the cellar. Getting closer and closer, I closed my eyes to wait with the dagger held out in front of me.

An electric pain engulfed my entire body, and I cried out. My scream bounced off the cellar walls. And everything went black.

33

Swanson

Swanson had never been so glad to see Hart in all his life. She stood over Randall with her arm still raised in the air, taser in hand. He lay on the floor, unconscious. She dug her foot into the side of his stomach. He didn't move.

"Shit, I think he's banged his head." She looked over at Swanson. "Oh my god he's chained you up like a frigging animal."

He tried to form words but his tongue wouldn't work. She ran over to him and pulled at the cuffs.

"What the fuck has he done? We'll need to find the key."

"Water," Swanson gasped and pointed at the bottle of water.

Hart grabbed it and opened it up. She sniffed the bottle and held it out for him to drink from, the pain in his head too much to manage without a drink. At least if it was poisoned Hart could get him to a hospital. The cool water soothed his throat and the pain in his head lessened. He jerked his head back and Hart put the water back down on the floor.

"Maybe he has a key on him," she said, returning to Dr Randall's motionless body.

"I think I can break these. They feel weak." Swanson finally made his tongue work now it didn't feel so much like sandpaper. He leant forward and pulled with all his strength.

"You'll still have cuffs round your wrists, you donut, hang on a minute." She fished through Randall's pockets and triumphantly held up a key a moment later.

"Hurry please," Swanson urged, pointing his head toward the cuffs.

She ran over and after a few seconds of fighting with the old locks she released the cuffs one by one.

"Thanks," Swanson managed, though it wasn't enough to convey his relief. "I'll get you lots of chocolate cake."

"Never mind that. Do you need a doctor?" she asked.

"Well, yeah. To get rid of the tumour," he replied with a grin.

She tutted. "Can't you ever be serious? I haven't got my handcuffs for him. Have you got cuffs?"

He shook his head. He took a deep breath and put both hands flat on the floor, pushing himself up. The blood rushed from his head and he swayed as he waited for it to pass. He felt Hart by his side and almost laughed at the thought of her trying to catch him. It only took a moment for his vision to restore, and the dizziness to pass. He turned to her. Her concerned face stared up at him, and he put a hand on each shoulder.

"Thank you for saving me from that fucking psychopath."

She smiled. "Wow, you can be serious. You owe me BIG! Like I am going to go on about this for a long time. I don't go about getting myself kidnapped like a damn damsel in distress, so god knows how you will make it up to me. Also, I don't think you're allowed to use the word psychopath anymore."

He laughed. "I will find a way to make it up to you. Don't worry. And yes, Summer would slap me if she heard me use that word. How did you know I was here?"

"I didn't, not at first. Summer called me. She had my number saved because apparently you gave it to her?"

"Yes, for emergencies."

"Well, I would say I'm not sure what you think would happen to her, but after all the shit that has happened, I'll let it pass. She said you called her, but when she answered she heard some sort of thud and the line went dead."

"I forgot all about calling her, actually."

"I called, and you didn't answer, so I went to your cottage. Your phone was on the drive, and your car door was unlocked. Talk about alarm bells with you and your bloody car. Anyway, a lady came over–"

"A lady?"

"Yes. She, er, she said she was your mother." Hart looked at him as if waiting for a reaction. He didn't give her one. "She said she'd been round once, but came back again. And as she rounded the corner she saw two people driving erratically in a van which had windows that were painted black, and I remembered we saw a van like that in the Adrenna car park. Plus, you didn't answer your door yet your car was there. She waited around to see if you'd gone for a walk but you didn't show."

"Oh, I see." Swanson wasn't sure what else to say.

"And I worried it was something to do with Dr Randall cos I read your text and obviously he didn't show up for his interview, so I came to Adrenna and saw the van in the car park."

"Fair enough. Did you speak to Glenda?"

"She wasn't there, someone is headed to her home address. But someone had propped the side door open, and weird wheel marks were made on the grass verge. So I knew something was going on. Something had been brought into the hospital on wheels. Listen, you know how you owe me one?" she said with pursed lips.

"Yes?"

"And saving your life is the best thing I could ever do for you, right?"

"Spit it out, Hart."

"I messed up." She winced and looked away.

He shrugged. "OK… tell me what you did and we'll fix it. It can't be that bad."

"Er… I let it slip to your mum about the tumour."

He sucked in a breath and looked away. "Well. That is a mistake."

"I know, I'm sorry. It just came out. I was speaking to her, and I said something like 'the tumour could have made you faint again.' i.e. the thud that she heard."

He let out his breath in a slow, controlled sigh. At least the decision about whether he told his mother he was ill was out of his hands. "Not to worry. It was an accident. It doesn't matter."

"Yeah. And I saved your life, so we're even, right?"

"Right. No chocolate cake for you though after that." Swanson pushed his mother to the back of his mind. He'd worry about her later. "Come on, let's sort out the good doctor."

He turned to check on Randall and saw a space where the doctor had lain. He went rigid and stepped back against the wall. The low light flickered, and shadows danced. The room was silent. He pulled Hart back against the wall next to him and peered around the cellar.

"Dr Randall," called out Hart, "please don't run away. It's OK. We'll look after you and get someone to check out your head."

"And you can tell me more about the devil," Swanson added through gritted teeth.

Footsteps came from the other side of the cellar. Swanson jumped forward and saw the dark outline of Dr Randall.

He was right next to the only exit.

Swanson ran. Hart was hot on his heels as they raced towards Dr Randall.

"Don't make the situation—argh."

A clash rang out from behind and Swanson turned. Hart was on the floor. She groaned in pain. Swanson stopped running.

"Are you OK?" He bent down to check on her.

"I've twisted my ankle, I think. Go get him quick. That door locks. It doesn't open from the inside without a key."

"Shit." Swanson leapt up from the floor and ran towards the door.

But Randall was already there. He gave Swanson a serious look.

"I'll tell Summer you said hi, and you two will be together soon," he said.

And he slammed the door behind him.

It took Swanson a few seconds to reach the door. He yanked on it with all his might but it was no use. Even with his strength the heavy steel door was not moving. He reached into his pocket for his phone, but it was empty. Where was the last time he'd seen his phone?

He had no way of warning Summer that Dr Randall was on his way.

34

Summer

Summer lay back in her hospital bed having eaten a mushy meal of fish pie and mashed potato. She felt nauseous as the food sat heavy in her stomach, and resting her head back on the soft pillow felt good. The nice pillows were one benefit of staying in the hospital.

The stay hadn't been as bad as she'd feared. Other than missing Joshua, it was almost nice to have a break from the mundaneness of life. Though it was hard to sleep at night in the noisy hospital, despite still being in her own private side room, and her eyes were so heavy now from lack of sleep and morphine, she couldn't keep them open. She closed them and thought of Joshua.

He wore his favourite dinosaur top in her reverie and laughed as he cuddled into her, his little body fitting perfectly with hers.

"Love you, Mummy," he said as he squeezed her far too tight.

"Love you more, baby," she replied.

A click of a door made them both glance up, and Summer opened her eyes. A tall man stood in front of her. He dressed like a doctor with the white coat and a badge around his neck, but not one she recognised.

"Hello there, Summer." A thick, dark stubble lined his smile. "I'm here to check up on you."

"Hi." Summer smiled back. "Sorry, I was so tired I couldn't help but close my eyes."

"Oh, that's OK. You need plenty of rest," the doctor said.

Summer smiled and waited for him to begin whatever it was he needed to do. Yet the doctor didn't move.

"Do you usually work on this ward?" she asked, breaking the awkward silence.

"No. I normally work with patients who have… more neurological disorders. I'm standing in due to short staffing."

"Oh, I see. I saw a doctor for a checkup before dinner, mind, an hour ago. He said everything was OK? So you can move on to someone else if you're busy," Summer said, hoping he would go away. There was an uncomfortable vibe emanating from him, though she wasn't sure why.

"Did you? Well, that's great. Let me check if they have filled your notes out and I'll be on my way."

The doctor moved to the foot of the bed and pulled Summer's folder of notes from the holder that was attached there. Summer watched his face. His right eye twitched. She looked over at the closed door. The staff never closed the door unless she asked. The man looked up at her and their eyes met. A chill ran through her. Whoever this was, she wasn't safe.

Her hand vibrated, and relief flooded her. She whipped out the phone from under the sheets and pressed the green answer button.

"Hi. baby," she smiled into the camera, "I'm here with the doctor, look." She pointed the camera at the doctor. She made sure the doctor realised he'd been seen in her room. Though it was by a child.

"Hi, doctor." Joshua waved into the camera.

The doctor's mouth was ajar, but he said nothing. He put up one hand in an awkward wave to Joshua.

Summer turned the camera back to her. "Get Daddy for a sec, hun," she said.

"Daaaaaaaad, come here." Joshua's voice rang out.

She braved a glance at the doctor. The way he stared at her made her want to run.

"Hey, you OK?" Joshua's dad, Richard, appeared on the camera.

"Hi, yes I'm doing OK, thanks. I wanted to say, can you call me back in five minutes? I'm here with the doctor, see?"

She pointed the camera at the doctor again and lingered on his face. He cleared his throat and looked down at her notes, pretending to be busy.

"Yes, sure. We'll call in five minutes. Speak soon." Richard gave a little wave and hung up.

Summer smiled sweetly at the doctor.

"So you're a mother?" he asked her slowly.

"Yes. Sorry about that. He gets really worried if I don't answer. We're very close! Don't know what he would have done if I hadn't made it."

The doctor put down her notes and stumbled backwards. "Oh, no problem. I can see your notes are fine, anyway. So I'll go now."

His hands were shaking, but he rushed off through the door before she said anything else. How strange. Was that her anxiety about being in hospital making it seem worse than it was? Or was he just a weird man? He left the door open, and

Summer saw her favourite nurse standing outside.

"Sally?" she called out, her voice breaking because of her sore throat.

Sally made her way into the room, sighing and smiling as she usually did. You could tell with one look Sally was born to be a nurse. Summer had never seen her in a bad mood.

"Yes, my cherub?" she asked. Despite only being about ten years older than Summer, you'd think she was her grandma by the way she acted.

"A quick one. Who was that doctor who just left my room?" Summer asked.

"Oh, the tall one? Yes, what was he doing in here?" She glanced behind her as if to check he wasn't standing outside the door.

"He said he was filling in because you're short staffed. He was strange, to be honest," Summer said.

"Well, yes, considering I'm pretty positive he works in neurology." Sally chewed on her lip, deep in thought.

"What would he be doing here?"

"Who knows with these doctors, love? They help each other out sometimes, though. Usually they would come and speak to us first at reception so we can tell them about the patients."

"What was his name? He didn't even say."

"Oh, that was Dr Tiffin." Sally smiled. "I'm sure it was nothing to worry about."

35

The Servant

I sat outside Derby Royal Hospital and took deep breaths in a vain attempt to soothe my banging heart beat. My pocket vibrated. He was calling me. My hands shook as I reached into my jeans pocket and pulled out the phone.

He was going to kill me.

"Hello?" My voice sounded strange and far away, as though it didn't belong to me, and instead it belonged below somewhere, the way it echoed up from the ground.

"What do you mean, you've locked the police officers in the basement?" His angry voice was so loud I had to hold the phone away from my ear.

"I didn't mean to! It was the woman's fault. That stupid cow snuck up on me. I'll show her." I clenched my fist and felt the sharpness of nails digging in against my flesh.

"I don't know why I trusted you with Swanson. You couldn't even kill the advocate. You need to fix this."

"I can't kill them both. I need you."

"You don't need to kill them. Let them out and let them arrest you. Do not mention my name."

My mouth fell open in horror. He didn't understand. "I can't let them go! I told you, the Devil needs Swanson. You know this."

"It doesn't matter now. You bring only women to me, *untouched*. And I give them to the Devil. Your only other job is to get rid of the body."

"No. I saw Him. I told you."

There was a pause before He sighed loudly. "That was in your head, James."

I scoffed. "How do you know which visions are in *my* head?"

"Because he talks to me properly. I'm not nuts like you are. Now go away and sort it out. Do not mention my name."

"No. They'll have no signal down there. They won't be able to call anyone. They'll get weak and–"

"And what, James? Die? What will the police do when two of their own are missing, and the last case they investigated was a stabbing at your hospital? The only reason I helped you get Swanson to your hospital was because he isn't someone I want looking into us. And if you did it by yourself you'd mess it up. And now you've messed it up, anyway. Yes, it would have been good to get Swanson out of the way. But I give the orders, not you, and now you've gotten caught."

My heart felt heavy as I realised the weight of his words. I had messed it up. If I got caught, I would no longer be of any use to Him. The only thing left to do would be to spread the word and tell everyone about my deeds. Recruitment might be my only survival.

"So the Devil will come for me?" It was more of a statement. I already knew it to be true.

"Yes, he will. You're in serious trouble."

"When will He come?"

"I don't know. But if you finish off the advocate, at least she can't talk anymore. Sally will let you in. Do it quickly. I tried but she's clever. She got me on camera. It's down to you now."

I hung up the phone. There was only one thing I could think to do. Kill everybody and run. That's the only way I might get away without going to prison and carry on doing what I was supposed to be doing for Him. The hospital loomed in front of me. It would easily intimidate most people. But not me. This was my domain. The advocate would be in there somewhere. Alone. Helpless. She started all this by not dying. Tonight, she will die first.

36

Swanson

Swanson continued to push all of his weight against the door, yet it barely budged. Adrenna was reminiscent of a time when such buildings were indestructible. One thing he knew for sure, he wasn't stepping foot in a fucking asylum ever again.

"It's not going to work. We need to be clever. I'm going to see if there are any signal spots at all. Sit tight. We'll get to Summer. Here's your phone, by the way. I saw it in your driveway." Hart limped over to him, wincing at her ankle.

Her words didn't have a reassuring effect, though he took his phone from her. He was grateful to be reunited with it, but there was no signal. Just a few missed calls and messages from Hart whilst it sat on his drive.

A scuttling noise echoed through the basement, and their heads whipped around to check out the sound. Short squeaks accompanied it and Hart looked at him in disgust with a shiver. She got her phone, turned the flashlight on and pointed it at the floor.

"Someone must know you're in here?" he said to Hart, "how

did you find me?"

"I told you. The door was left propped open and Glenda was gone. I walked around the side of her office where Randall took us last time." She shuddered. "It was creepy. And I went to his office looking for him. Remember that door we saw there last time?"

"Yes." He motioned for her to continue.

"Well, that leads to some stairs, which lead to that door." She pointed at the steel door in front of them. "And a book held it open."

He studied the door and noted the cracks of light around the loose fitting top. He looked around for something that he could at least hit it with to make some noise and draw attention. If they were in Adrenna, there must be staff around in the wards at least. Maybe even Aaron. There wasn't much in the cellar. There were bars that ran from floor to ceiling, the remnants of old cells. He spotted a few more old shackles, though most were rusted or broken. He walked through the middle of the cellar, what he imagined must have been the corridor originally, and turned on the flashlight on his phone. The third 'cell' down had the most gaps in its bars, and broken metal tubes lay on the floor. Bingo. He grabbed a metal bar from the floor and ran towards the main basement door. Hart leant against the wall, with her bad foot in the air. She looked disdainfully at the metal bar.

"If it's sound proof no one's going to hear it, are they?" she asked.

"If there's light the sound will travel." He pointed at the crack in the door. "Stand back and cover your ears."

She raised an eyebrow at him, but took a few steps back and held both hands to her ears without arguing. Swanson held the metal bar high in the air behind him and brought it crashing down onto the steel door. The clashing noise echoed off every surface in the cellar and made Hart wince. He did it again, and again, until Hart couldn't take it anymore.

"Stop!" she yelled, "for one minute. It's too much."

"Just for a minute." Swanson's own ears were ringing. They might both be deaf by the time they got out. At least they'd be alive, though. As the ringing in his ears slowed, another sound caught Swanson's attention.

Slow footsteps. A flash of darkness against the crack of light in the door. Someone was standing outside the basement.

Instead of letting them out, the person was pacing. Swanson nudged Hart to get her attention, and once she looked up, he pointed to the moving light behind the doorway. Her eyes widened.

"Hello?" she yelled out.

The movement stopped, the unknown figure frozen.

"Can you let us out please?" Hart tried again.

The pair stood deathly still, but there was no response from the figure outside.

Hart looked at Swanson and shrugged. She stepped closer to him, gingerly putting her sore foot down on the ground.

"Maybe it's Dr Randall?" she whispered to him.

"I doubt it. I bet he's done a runner. Surely. Any sane person would," he whispered back.

"He's not sane though, is he?" she replied.

"Hello? It's the police here. Please open this door at once." Swanson tried with the unknown person.

"Detective Inspector Swanson?" Came a woman's voice. It sounded familiar. He racked his brain trying to figure out who it was. Hart stared at him with wide eyes.

"It's that receptionist," she whispered.

"His grandma? Stay quiet," he whispered to Hart. He raised his voice to speak to Glenda. "Hi, yes, is that Glenda? Can you open the door, please?"

Silence filled the air once more, and Swanson's heart deflated. She wasn't going to let them out.

Would she help Dr Randall?

"I can't." Came Glenda's beaten voice eventually. "I am sorry, Officer Swanson. But I have to protect my grandson."

"You can call me Alex. Why does leaving us in here protect him?" Swanson tried to make his voice sound friendly and neutral.

"You will take him away. But he isn't well," Glenda stated simply. "He needs someone to keep an eye on him."

"I agree. We can help look after him, you know."

"I'm not sure anyone can help him while he listens to his devil friend. He's just like his father, unfortunately. And I won't let my grandson end up in a place like Adrenna. The so-called care is appalling."

He bit his tongue at the irony of her calling the hospital run by her crazy grandson appalling.

"Tell me about his father?" Swanson asked. He got a nudge in the chest from Hart, but he put his finger to his lips for her to be patient. Glenda might let them go, if he could just convince her he cared.

"He was a troubled soul. It all stemmed from his dad, Dr Randall's grandfather. My husband met a tragic end in this very hospital after visions of seeing the devil. And the devil told him to do terrible things. He killed a woman here. A nurse. And he killed himself two weeks later. He couldn't live with the guilt. Our son, Dr Randall's dad, suffered after that.

A few years later, he told me the devil had been passed to him. That he saw it, too. And he met the same fate. James was the one who broke the curse."

Swanson tried not to snort. He obviously hadn't broken the so-called curse at all. "He broke the curse? How?" he asked instead.

"Yes. He was fine all his life. A couple of years ago, he started going downhill. He made a new friend. Another doctor who tried to help him, but he kept getting worse."

"How so?"

"This Dr Tiffin gave him medicine to help, but it made him worse and now he only believes Dr Tiffin. He doesn't listen to me at all. I hope you don't think he's done anything to harm anyone. He wouldn't, you know."

Dr Tiffin? Swanson's head span. He tried to focus on what to say next. To focus on getting out and protecting Summer. He clenched his jaw.

"I don't know what he's done at the moment, Glenda. But you need to let us out so he doesn't have two dead police officers to worry about. And if you don't do it soon, another nurse might be killed and I won't be able to save him from that."

Again, there was silence. The shadow under the door didn't move. Swanson counted slowly to thirty. Still no response.

"Glenda?" he breathed.

He heard the jangling sound of keys, and the shadow moved. Hart looked at him with her hand in a prayer position and he tried not to laugh. He got Summer's number ready to dial as soon as he had signal. He needed to warn her, and he had to be quick.

37

Summer

Sally picked up Summer's medical notes from the caged box at the bottom of the bed. The same notes that were in the hands of Dr Tiffin moments before. She stood, tapping one foot off the floor as she flicked through the file.

"Hmm. He doesn't seem to have written anything," she mused.

"Can you make sure he doesn't come in again, please?" Summer asked.

"Well, I don't exactly have the authority to keep a doctor out. You look tired. Are you in pain?" Sally threw her a sympathetic look. She moved around to the side of Summer's bed and increased the morphine dose through her intravenous catheter in the back of her hand. The sleeve of her uniform lifted as she reached up, and Summer spotted yellow bruising around her wrist. "But I can promise to let you know if he returns."

Summer nodded. "Thank you. I know it's silly to be wary of a doctor. There was something weird about the way he looked at me."

Sally cocked her head to one side and sucked on her lip. After a moment, she said, "I'll tell him you're sleeping if he comes back. I won't let him in here unless I'm with him, OK?"

"Yes! Thank you, Sally. That would be great." Summer smiled gratefully.

Sally smiled back. "No problem, my duck. You go get some sleep now, OK?" She walked over to the door and turned to give Summer a wink before stepping out of the room, firmly closing the door behind her.

Summer smiled to herself and settled back into the soft pillows. Sally made her feel much safer. Her eyes were heavy with sleep as the increased morphine ran through her veins like a smooth blanket being pulled over her body. The room was far too quiet now the door was closed, and she found herself unable to relax even with the extra dosage. She flicked on the TV and an old episode of Time Team flashed up. Her heart leapt at the sight of her dad's favourite TV show. She'd always moaned when it came on as a child.

'Why can't we watch Sabrina, Daddy?'

But he'd say it was time for adult TV now and she'd cuddle up with him, anyway. He'd stroke her hair and she would take a nap, listening to the music and droning voices as she fell asleep. She wished he was here now, stroking her hair once more.

The familiar dull ache in her chest appeared, and she swallowed back a lump in her throat. She closed her eyes and focused on the familiar music and chatter of the Time Team crew, lost in memories, oblivious to her phone vibrating, or the creaking of her bedroom door as a quiet hand slowly pushed it open.

38

The Servant

I stalked through the hospital, not stopping to say hello to anyone. I kept my head down, sweat dripping from my forehead. Derby was a large hospital, and most staff didn't even give me a second glance. They assumed I was a doctor that belonged there. I took the stairs all the way, not wanting to be stuck in a lift with people who might spot the beads of sweat or the shake of my hands.

I knew where the High Dependency Unit was from my time as a junior doctor in the hospital years ago. It had changed little since, if at all. I pressed the buzzer and waited for the nurse to let me in. It didn't take long for a plump young nurse with thick black hair to arrive at the door.

"Oh, hello. Are you here to see any particular patient?" She smiled up at me, her accent rough. I spotted the top of a tattoo peeking through the top of her uniform on her chest.

"Hello, no, I'm here to fill in for someone. Can't remember his name." I smiled widely, certain she was going to see through my lie. To my relief, she waved me inside. Another nurse stalked over. She was older than the tattoo lady.

"I'll take it from here, thanks Bella," she said, and motioned for me to follow her to the reception desk.

"Right you are, Sally," Bella replied, and walked off in the other direction.

"I'm here for Summer?" I said to the nurse in a low voice.

"Yes, I know. Come here." She led me to a small private room off the left of the initial entrance to the ward.

"We recently moved her to this room because she's doing so well. She'll be out of this ward tomorrow," Sally said in a strange warning tone.

"Yes, alright. I know I messed up," I whispered back.

"Shh! Not here." She pushed open Summer's door and shoved me inside before anyone saw. She stepped in behind me.

"I increased her morphine dose. She'll be flat out so go do what you need to do and be quick," she demanded.

I stood open-mouthed for a moment. The last time I'd seen Sally Tiffin she'd been quiet and sweet. She was certainly taking a leaf out of her husband's book.

"Go on." She nodded at Summer and stepped out of the room. She swiftly closed the door tight behind her.

And it was Summer and me alone at last. Well, almost alone. The TV blasted out and interrupted my thoughts. I grabbed the remote from her bedside table and flicked it off. Silence.

Her head had almost disappeared into the pillow she'd sunk so far into it. Her skin was so pale it would soon match the white pillow. I watched her chest move up and down rhythmically for a moment. The rhythm calmed my own breathing, and I ran two fingers across the back of her hand. She did nothing. I wrapped my fingers around her hand and squeezed it tight. Still, nothing. Sally really had dosed her up.

So I continued to run my fingers up along her arm. The sparse little hairs rose at my touch, and goosebumps raised up as if she was excited to be touched by me. Maybe she knew what was going to happen to her. Maybe she already understood how lucky she was.

I traced one finger up her neck and across her cheek. Her skin was soft and smooth. And I knew what I was doing was the right thing. She would be a delight for the Devil.

I ran my finger back down her neck, to her chest, and caressed one breast. Still, she didn't move. I squeezed, watching her face for any signs of her waking. She didn't even flinch.

She was mine for the taking. I wrapped my fingers around the top of her hospital gown to pull it down.

But a growl stopped me in my tracks. It came out of nowhere and pierced my brain and I heard nothing else. I bent over, both hands flew up to my head to cover my ears.

The Devil was here.

And He wasn't happy.

39

Swanson

Swanson rang Summer again as he raced across the gravel car park to Hart's red car, but there was still no answer. God damn it. How could she be too busy to answer her phone in the hospital? Maybe he was already too late.

"Throw me your keys," he shouted at Hart.

"No way!" she yelled back, running behind him despite her weak ankle.

He stopped and turned around to face her. She also stood still and bent over, wincing at the pain in her ankle. "Now, Hart. I need to get to Summer before he does, and he had a pretty big head start. Come here."

She reluctantly pulled her keys out of her pocket and threw them at him as he walked towards her. He took hold of her arm and helped her to hurry to the car.

"I'll call the hospital," she said as he helped her into the passenger seat.

Swanson jumped into the driver's seat and raced out of the car park. Hart clung on to the handle above the door.

"Don't kill us both trying to get to her," she mumbled as she grabbed some spare cuffs out of the glove compartment.

Swanson ignored her as he flew down the country lane to get into the city. They'd make it in ten minutes if he was quick, and if nobody got in their way. Hart called the hospital and asked them to check on Summer and call her back asap, as well as calling for some backup in case Randall was indeed at the hospital.

Swanson made it to the hospital in eight minutes, abandoning Hart's car on the side of the entrance. The hospital hadn't yet called them back, and so the pair raced up to the high dependency unit, Swanson out in front and Hart still hobbling behind him. They ignored the stares and open mouths of sickly patients and staff in their blue uniforms. Swanson didn't stop for breath until he reached the buzzer for the ward. Hart was nowhere to be seen.

A few seconds passed by, and no one came to the door. He banged on the glass of the door instead. A nurse stalked over to the door. She put a finger to her lips and narrowed her eyes. He recognised her from before, nurse Sally. He flashed his ID against the glass of the door.

"You need to calm down please, Sir," she shouted through the door, her arms crossed.

He did not have time for some random nurse's tantrum.

"This is an emergency. Let me in now or you will be arrested," he yelled.

Her narrow eyes widened, and she took a step back. Her hand flew up to the release button on the wall, and the door buzzed open as Hart caught up with him. Swanson pushed open the door and Hart followed closely behind. He ran through the ward to the small private room at the other end, but as he pushed open the door, his heart fell through his stomach.

Her bed was empty.

He turned to see a different nurse standing behind him with wavy black hair, looking up at him with wide eyes.

"Where is Summer Thomas?" he demanded.

"Summer's been moved down there." She pointed to the other end of the ward. "On the right near the entrance."

Swanson moved before the nurse finished her sentence, but Hart was already halfway down the ward. Her ankle must have felt better because she darted to the other end and careened straight into nurse Sally and another doctor. Sally had her hand on the doctor's elbow and was dragging him towards the exit. She let go as soon as Hart ran into them, but he was certain of what he'd seen.

"Hart, that's Randall!" he yelled.

Randall cried out in fear and put his hands to his face as if he thought Hart was going to hurt him. Hart jumped up and grabbed Randall's arm, pushing him up against the wall. He didn't fight with her, but he sobbed. His wails rang out through the ward as Hart pulled his wrists behind his back and cuffed him. She sat him down firmly in a chair near the reception desk, and he continued to sob quietly.

Swanson looked at Sally. "Show me where Summer is," he demanded.

Her eyes were wide and brimmed with tears, her whole body tremoured. She lifted one hand and pointed to a door right next to them.

"You come with me," Swanson said, grabbing her skinny arm and dragging her with him to the room. She didn't argue. He felt her shake under his touch, but until he found Summer, he didn't care.

But as they entered the ward, he threw Sally to one side and heaved. Summer was in bed, nestled between the thick sheet and pillow.

Her pure white sheet stained red with blood.

40

Swanson

Summer's skin was translucent against the shine of the bright hospital lights. Intense voices echoed around the room from the ward, but Swanson ignored it. He pushed Sally into a chair in the corner and dashed towards Summer.

"Don't move," he ordered as he turned to check on Summer, and put one hand against her neck to check her pulse. As he moved his hand across her face, he felt her warm breath tickle his fingers. The sick feeling in his stomach dared to lift.

"Summer?" He whipped off the blood stained duvet. Where was the blood coming from? She lay in pale pink pyjamas. They weren't stained or torn. He saw no blood anywhere on her body.

"It's not her blood," Sally said, sucking in a deep breath, "it's his. She's sedated with morphine. She's fine."

She put a hand to her mouth and sobbed quietly.

"It's 'his'? Who do you mean? Dr Randall?" Swanson asked.

Sally pointed under the hospital bed, and for the first time, Swanson looked down and noticed a small river of blood converging at the tip of the bed. He'd been too worried about Summer to notice much of anything else. He bent down and almost toppled back, unprepared for the sight that awaited him.

Dr Tiffin lay under the bed on his back. His skin was pale, and his face contorted into a scream. Swanson's nausea returned. That image would not disappear from his brain for a while. He took a breath, reached out and checked the doctor's pulse. But his skin was ice cold, his eyes wide open and unblinking.

"He's dead," Sally sobbed. "I already tried to save him."

"What the hell was he doing in here? Dr Tiffin doesn't work on this ward." He stood up and turned to face Sally.

"They knew each other for years, from med school apparently, though they've been best mates for a couple of years." She put her head down and sobbed hard.

"Listen, Sally. I don't know what you've gotten yourself involved with here, but you need to start talking. Tell me what happened. Is anyone else in danger?"

She shook her head and took a deep breath. "I'm Nick's wife."

"And Nick is Dr Tiffin, right?" Swanson asked.

"Yes, He tried to pretend to be the devil. He was trying to talk James out of killing Summer, but James got confused. I don't know what really happened. He pulled out a knife and stabbed Nick." she collapsed into tears again.

"You're going to need to come with us to the station, Sally,"

Swanson stepped back to the ward door to check on Hart. She stood above Randall, who was still sitting at reception with his cuffs on. He sat quietly and made no fuss. Hart was on the phone and looked up at Swanson to give him a thumbs up.

At that moment, a buzzer rang out and Swanson looked over at the door. Backup had arrived, and several uniformed officers stood outside the door.

* * *

Two officers took Randall and Sally away to the police station for questioning, whilst Swanson and Hart stayed behind to await forensics for Dr Tiffin.

"Have they moved Summer?" asked Hart as they sat outside the room where the body lay two hours later.

"Yes, she was a bit disorientated, to be honest. Not sure she had a clue what was happening."

"Christ. How much morphine did they give her? What a day." Hart exhaled slowly.

Swanson nodded, unable to add anything useful to her conclusion.

"We need to speak to all these nurses and patients," he looked over at her. "Question them all. See what they saw."

"Yeah, we do." Hart agreed.

He looked around the ward. Many patients lay in open beds, with no real clue as to the drama that unfolded around them. There were three open wards, with eight beds in each, plus six private side rooms. Doctors, nurses, health care assistants and other staff all milled around assisting patients.

"There's quite a lot of them," he sighed.

"Yes, there are." Hart nodded.

Neither one moved. They continued to allow the hustle and bustle to happen around them. Swanson's headache had returned with a vengeance, but he'd left his pills at home. He rested his head against the wall and tried to focus through the pain on what had happened tonight between Randall and Tiffin.

"Coffee first," Hart said eventually, "want anything?"

Swanson shook his head. "I'll wait here. There are a few things I need to get my head around before we ask questions."

She got up and walked away towards the kitchen that the nurses had allowed them access to, and Swanson considered what they knew so far. Randall killed Tiffin. They knew each other, and somehow Sally got involved. But if Sally was so upset with Randall for murdering her husband, why was she trying to help Randall get out of the ward? It still didn't make any sense. Somehow, he had to find the missing piece of the puzzle.

41

Swanson

Twenty-four hours later Swanson nestled into his favourite corner of the sofa. His thinking space. Usually, after catching a culprit he would feel lighter, elated even that he won the chase. Yet his mind was full of questions. None of it made any sense.

Why had Sally not screamed the place down when Randall killed Tiffin, her husband? And if she'd tried to revive him, how come she wasn't covered in blood?

The buzz of his phone ringing tickled his leg, pulling him out of his thoughts. He checked the caller ID before answering, Hart.

"I'm done with Glenda," she said, "she knows he has visions involving the devil but vehemently denies he's done anything to hurt anyone or that she killed Stockport's first wife. She didn't really want visitors in the hospital because of it, though."

"True protective grandma style?"

"Yep. So she was no help, really. But we've got Sally in soon, so that will be interesting."

"Mmm. I was thinking about why she would help Randall

clean up the room and escape after murdering her husband." Swanson peered out of his window. Right at the spot Randall had knocked him out. He supposed it was Tiffin who helped him. He needed someone stronger than Sally. But why would Tiffin have wanted to hurt Swanson, unless he really did see the devil too?

"Yes, it is strange. I know Tiffin was giving Randall medicines to help him with his visions, but Glenda said he got worse, and so did his erratic behaviour."

"Well, yes. He did murder a nurse *and* a doctor, attempt to murder an advocate and a police officer. He's clearly not all there, but he is sane enough to make plans and hide what he was doing. Quite ingenious for someone whose mental health is so poor their thoughts must be all over the place." Swanson thought aloud. "Funny really, because my own symptoms were also worse after taking Dr Tiffin's prescription medicine."

Hell, the dizziness never even occurred until he'd started taking the tablets. And there was that damn old man he kept seeing. He actually felt better in the last 24 hours from not taking them.

Wait a minute. He really did feel better for not taking them.

"I'll call you back in a minute, Hart," he said, jumping up off the sofa.

He pulled out the pills the doctor had given him and read the side of the bottle. He hadn't bothered before with so much else on his mind, but kicked himself now. The label on the side read:

Tramadol.

Hmm.

That seemed normal enough. He'd definitely heard of Tramadol, though it wasn't something he'd taken before. He brought up Google to check it out and clicked on to the NHS website. The side effects listed were dizziness, nausea, headaches... the list went on.

His eyes flicked down to serious side effects. Extreme dizziness. Hallucinations. Seeing or hearing things that aren't there.

The man with white eyes? Was that what he was?

He checked the dosage of the pills. The label read as 50mg tablets. He pulled out one long, oval-shaped pill and peered at it. It looked like the image of a white tablet on the screen in front of him, but as he leaned in he realised the number on the pill said 400mg. A lot more than 50mg.

He checked the standard dosages on the NHS site. 50mg was the normal measure for pain that comes and goes. Which is what Swanson's pain did.

The 400mg tablets were slow release, and should be taken once a day only, starting off at 100mg a day until your body got used to it.

Well, Dr Tiffin never mentioned that. Why would he not mention that? Swanson had been taking two at a time. Unless he wanted Swanson to be disoriented?

But *why* would he want Swanson to feel like that? He grabbed his phone to give Hart a call.

"Hello Mr yes I'm just going to randomly hang up," she grumbled.

"Sorry about that. Listen, Dr Tiffin gave me some medicine for pain relief. He said to take a couple of tablets whenever I needed it. It turns out it's 400mg of slow release Tramadol. He either made a very unlikely mistake or he's been spiking me."

"What? And I thought he was the good doctor?"

"So did I, but there you go. And a mistake this big by someone with his vast experience seems extremely unlikely, doesn't it?"

"Well, I was going to tell you before you hung up that I had a quick chat with Randall, and he's started to talk. He blamed Tiffin mostly. He said Tiffin was like some kind of great messenger and Randall had to do what he said. Tiffin told him to get a woman and bring her to him alive. I wasn't really believing him but if Tiffin has been spiking you, then yes, he's possibly our second bad guy."

"Did he say anything else?"

"Yes. He said he chose the nurse, and he brought her to Tiffin who murdered her. Randall picked up the body and dumped it. But Tiffin said the devil told him Randall touched the body first. She'd already been raped, so she was no good and Randall needed to get another one. Someone more… *pure*."

"Hence him trying to stab Summer?" Swanson asked.

"Yep, hence Summer. He thought if he did it on the ward, someone else would take the body away, she'd go to the devil, and he wouldn't be tempted to, er, play with her."

A shot of nausea put an end to Swanson's hungry stomach.

"Anyway, Tiffin told him that he needed a strong man to protect Summer in the afterworld when he was busy, and Tiffin told him all about you."

"Why would Tiffin want me dead, though? Unless he really was crazy, too." Swanson put his head in his hands and racked his brain.

"You definitely don't know him?"

"No. Never met him until the hospital. I mean, he looked vaguely familiar but he had one of those faces I think."

"OK. Well, we'll see what happens today. Now piss off and get some sleep. You still have a tumour, you know."

After she hung up, Swanson moved into the kitchen to fix a

cheese and pickle sandwich to cure his rumbling stomach. He felt much better from not taking those damn tablets. He sat at his tiny dinner table, which had two chairs slotted underneath it in a perfect oval. His random Ikea purchase on the second day of living in the cottage. He tucked into his sandwich and reflected on his first meeting with Dr Tiffin. He had felt familiar now as he looked back, but he'd been too preoccupied with worry to think about it.

He picked up his second sandwich, but it fell back to the plate as the memory hit him. That was not the first time he'd met Tiffin.

And he realised why he'd told Randall to kill him.

42

The Servant

I sat alone in the interview room. The door was open, and an officer they called 'Forest' was standing right outside. My solicitor had gone to get a drink. I hadn't seen the Devil since yesterday. His presence was gone and Tiffin was dead. I wouldn't get my messages anymore. They only happened around Tiffin or after he'd given me a message. He gave me special pills too, so I could see the Devil myself. An ache tugged at my heart as I realised that without my pills, I wouldn't see a thing.

I didn't want to kill Tiffin, but the Devil insisted once Tiffin told me to leave Summer alone. He stood tall and powerful behind Tiffin and told me what to do. Being so trusting of my service to him, Tiffin hadn't flinched as I drove the knife into his heart. Sally told me I did the right thing. She was correct, of course. I hadn't had a choice. I had to do as I was told. But the police wouldn't see it that way. I knew.

Especially Swanson.

I looked up as footsteps echoed through the corridor. It was Hart. I knew by the way her heels hit the floor. But this time there was someone with her. Her face was cool as she walked in, but I could tell she wasn't happy about something. Behind her came DI Swanson. I'd grown quite fond of him. I saw why the Devil wanted him.

He didn't look too happy either, but I hadn't seen him smile once. I'm not sure he smiled all that often.

"Dr Randall, you remember my colleague, Detective Inspector Swanson?" DI Hart asked as she pulled the chair across from me over the tiles with a loud scrape. I shuddered at the noise.

I nodded and turned my attention to Swanson instead. He took the other chair adjacent to me and nodded a hello. My solicitor, Bobby Jones, followed them into the room and sat down next to me, the chair creaking under his considerable weight. The smell of Bobby's cheap cologne filled the room and stuck in my nostrils. I cleared my throat to keep away the nausea it gave me. He looked more like a pub landlord than a solicitor.

I waited for Hart to formally start recording and introduce the interview and smiled patiently at them both, but focused on Swanson as he talked.

"Dr Randall, can you tell me how you knew Dr Tiffin please?" he asked, his pen and notepad ready in front of him. He seemed far more interested in what I had to say than DI Hart.

I leant forward. "Of course. I really do want to help, Sir. I've known him for years. We went to medical school together in Nottingham."

"And how did you become friends?" he asked.

I sat back and sighed. I was going to have to go into more detail here than I originally thought to get him to understand what he could have been a part of. There was still a chance the

Devil would come back to me if I proved myself worthy. If I convinced Swanson to give himself up.

"Well, we shared most of the same classes, and for the first year we shared a dorm. Our bedrooms were on the same floor. We both kept away from most other students. I was a bit shy, and the other students were so stupid. Always getting drunk and being loud and acting like animals really. They didn't take anything seriously. Tiffin was the same as me. He liked to keep himself to himself. He was always out doing something or other, but always alone. In the second year, we moved into a flat together and shared the bills. We became quite good friends and opened up to each other. It turned out our families were… special."

"Your grandma said you only became friends a couple of years ago," Swanson said.

I stifled a laugh. I could never have told Grandma about Tiffin back then. "No. You know what grandmas are like. She never met him whilst I was at university. She never visited the flat. Tiffin and I lost touch after we graduated, and he got back in touch a couple of years ago via social media."

"You don't strike me as the type to be active on social media," DI Hart piped up.

"I'm not, but I am on work related media for my career." I didn't bother looking at her, and kept my gaze on DI Swanson instead.

"And why did he get back in touch?" he asked.

"He needed help with something. We met up for a coffee. The thing is, I helped him with something once before in university." I hesitated. It felt strange to say these words after keeping it a secret for so long.

"You don't have to answer," Bobby piped up. I glanced at

him with disdain and wished he would go away.

"We'd really appreciate anything you can tell us, Dr Randall," Swanson said, "you said you wanted to help us?"

"OK. Yes, yes, I do want to help *you*, Detective Inspector Swanson." I pointed at him to ensure he understood my meaning. He nodded for me to continue. "When we had our own flat, a year into living together, he had an accident with a young girl. Well, she would have been our age roughly at the time. She was about 19, we were 20ish. He'd taken her out and they'd come back to ours for… you know… things." I waved a hand.

"Sex?" DI Hart suggested.

Trust her to have no shame.

I nodded and swallowed. "Yes. That. She had *asked* him to choke her, and so he did. She kept asking for it and suddenly she wasn't breathing. He was in a complete mess over it. He could barely breathe. His life ruined because of one stupid girl."

"You don't need to say anything more, Dr Randall," Bobby grunted, his face looking sweaty and pale.

"What about her life?" DI Hart asked, her disdain obvious.

I closed my eyes and took a deep breath, washing away the irritation she brought about in me. I looked at her for the first time since the interview began.

"The whole thing was her fault. She *asked* him, remember?" I explained again.

"Do you really believe that?" she asked, her eyes narrowing.

"Of course I do," I scoffed, "there were no secrets between Dr Tiffin and I."

The clear memory of the perfectly formed, naked girl spread out on Tiffin's bed suddenly hit me like a brick. I closed my eyes and cleared my throat, trying to think of something else to focus on to push away the memory of the first girl I'd ever seen naked.

"Are you OK, Dr Randall?" Swanson's voice broke through my thoughts.

I opened my eyes again and focused on his face. The memory faded into a wisp of an image. I kept focused on his beard and nodded.

"OK. So what happened after he told you he'd murdered a young girl?" Swanson looked at me. He scribbled notes on his pad as he spoke.

"When the girl accidentally killed herself, you mean? Well, like I said, he was in a mess. Couldn't breathe properly. I calmed him down, and told him I would sort it out." I took a deep breath and closed my eyes. Talking about this was harder than I thought it would be. I wanted to be back there before everything went wrong. Me and her alone. She lay there quietly, eyes closed, while I explored her. She was beautiful. I opened my eyes. They were staring at me, patiently hanging on to every word.

"I went into the room, and dressed her as best I could and wrapped her up nicely in bin bags. Rigor mortis was settling in at that point, but I knew we only had a couple of hours before it set in properly. Luckily it was 2am and our flat was in a very quiet part of town. There were no cameras. Tiffin had checked that before we moved in. He didn't like being watched. He helped me put her in the back seat and I drove to a park nearby so police could find her easily."

"That was nice of you," DI Swanson said.

I nodded, glad he understood.

"I wanted her family to find her, but when I got there I

realised they needed to know what she'd done, too. They needed to realise it was *her* fault that she was dead. I made it clear by cutting off the bin bag and clothes and burning them a few days later."

DI Hart cleared her throat. She didn't understand like DI Swanson did. "Weren't you worried about being caught?" she asked.

"No. Tiffin said the Devil would protect us, and he did. Although that wasn't his name back then." I wondered if he would understand the Devil was real now. I couldn't understand much from his face. DI Swanson must be amazing at poker.

"Sorry? That wasn't the devil's name?" DI Swanson asked.

"What? No. It wasn't Tiffin's name. His name was Billy." I saw Swanson's eyes widen, though his set jaw gave nothing away. "Why?"

"What was his surname?" he asked.

"It was Logan. Billy Logan."

He cleared his throat, and I noticed the subtle clench of his jaw.

"And you left the girl in which park?" Hart asked.

"Grosvenor Park."

"And when did this happen again?" Swanson asked.

"Well, I think that's all I want to say right now." I sighed. They didn't seem to understand like I'd hoped so far.

"OK. So can I ask, before university, did you live at Adrenna? I'm confused about your family background. It's quite a tragic story," DI Swanson asked.

"Yes. I realise you don't know about the Devil. You haven't had the pleasure of being chosen by Him. But all the men in my family have had that. It isn't tragic at all." I shrugged.

"Let's start with your grandad's first wife. She died in 1981. What happened?" he asked.

"My Grandad took her for the Devil. He did panic and make up some story about a burglar, but he did a very noble thing in giving up his love for Him. She was the first in our family to go. But after giving her up, he couldn't bring himself to kill anyone else, and the Devil sentenced him to live for ten years without her before trying again. Though he met and married Glenda within a year. Ten years later, Grandad killed a nurse the devil chose for him, and he tried to kill a male patient to protect the nurse, but he failed with the patient, and couldn't take his failure. He killed himself."

"Quite the story," muttered DI Hart, "and your dad?"

"Yes. It's incredible, really. It quite troubled my dad as a boy. He got into a lot of issues at school and ended up being home schooled. He lived on the top floor of Adrenna. And Grandad would tell him all about the Devil. He passed his gift to my dad when he died, but the Devil made him wait ten years to make sure he was worthy. He killed a nurse chosen by the Devil, and instead of killing a male patient, he got greedy. The nurse was the one he wanted to be with. He wanted to be the one to protect her, so he killed himself."

"And where is your mum in all of this?" DI Swanson asked.

"I have no idea." I looked away and shifted in the chair. "Can I have a glass of water, actually?"

The whereabouts of my mother was one thing I was not prepared to share, even with DI Swanson. I looked around for her nervously. She liked to appear when I was in trouble. But I would take what happened to her to my grave, no matter what she did to make me tell.

43

Swanson

Two days later Swanson and Hart sat outside Adrenna for the last time. Swanson had driven and the pair still sat in his Audi in the bleak car park. Neither were in a particular hurry to return to Adrenna. The temperature was still cool despite the sky brightening and the clouds giving way to strong beams of sunlight, which bounced off the foreboding turrets and made the usual eerie atmosphere of Adrenna appear a bit lighter

"It doesn't seem as..." Swanson paused, struggling to find the right word as he unbuckled his seat belt.

"Scary?" Hart suggested.

"Just not as atmospheric or something." He pushed open the car door and climbed out, the sun surprisingly warm on his face. Hart climbed out too and met him at the bonnet of his car. The pair crossed their arms and looked up at Adrenna as other officers arrived around them.

"Well, we do know most of her secrets now," Hart said, "maybe it's the mystery that's gone."

Swanson nodded slowly. "Yeah, I think that's it. Come on.

Let's get this over with and find out any last secrets."

They stalked down to the side door of Adrenna and two separate groups of six officers followed behind them. Adrenna was a big place, and the warrant Swanson held was for private areas of the hospital which were not occupied by patients. He shuddered at the thought of the dark basement where Randall had shackled him. He would not be the one searching down there, that's for sure. Anyway, whatever was hiding on the top floor was probably more interesting.

Glenda was not on the reception desk today, and instead a junior nurse had taken on the role of receptionist temporarily. She let Swanson and the other officers straight in as soon as she saw them on the camera, and greeted them in the corridor with a cheery smile as he explained the warrant, and that they needed access to non-patient areas of the hospital.

"I've been expecting you. Aaron is going to show you where you need to go," she beamed.

"Oh, OK. That would be great." Swanson tried not to show his shock at how easy it had been to get access. The team walked through into the reception area where Aaron was waiting. He nodded at Swanson and gave a perfunctory, brief smile.

"I hear you're going to give us a tour of the non-patient occupied parts of the hospital?" Swanson asked him.

"Yes, though I haven't seen all of them myself, so we'll be exploring together a little." He shrugged and gave Swanson an apologetic glance. "We'll start in the offices though, if that's OK."

Aaron led them through to the back of the reception where Dr Randall had taken them a few days prior.

"I'll need his office first, Aaron," Swanson said, "take this first team to the door that's in there. The basement."

"I didn't realise there was a basement," Aaron replied with a frown.

"Yes, in Randal's office, through the door within," Swanson motioned for the first team of 6 officers to follow Aaron and stood to one side to let them through. "Make sure you keep the door open with something heavy."

Aaron reappeared a couple of minutes later, looking paler than he had done.

"Are you OK?" Swanson asked.

"Er, yes. Yes. Fine."

"Bit of a sight down there, isn't it?"

Aaron nodded and swallowed before raising his head to look Swanson in the eye. "Where do you need to go next?"

"The third floor. What's up there, by the way?"

Aaron shrugged. "I've never been up there. I haven't actually worked here that long. After all of this, it is time to move on again. I don't seem to have much luck with these places. But I opened that door by accident once when I was trying to find Dr Randall." He motioned to the door across from Randall's office. "And Dr Randall suddenly turned up behind me. He was weirdly annoyed that I'd opened the door."

Aaron opened up the door and jerked his head for Swanson to look. It was a small, square space, the only purpose of which seemed to be to hide the stairs going up to the third floor.

Aaron went first, huffing by the time he got halfway. Swanson's chest felt tight, but he took slow, deep breaths and refused to appear out of breath to anyone. Particularly Hart, who had watched him like a hawk since learning about the tumour.

At the top, Aaron took out his set of his keys and attempted to unlock the door. The key didn't work, so he tried the next one. And the next one. Before eventually turning to look at Swanson with pink cheeks.

"Sorry, I don't know what to do if it's none of these keys. They're the only keys I have. These are the same keys all nurses get."

"It's OK. We can break it down if we have to," Swanson said, looking warily at how thick the door appeared, and at the small space of the stairway. "But let's see if we can find a key first."

"If you were Randall, where would you hide the key?" Hart looked up at Swanson.

He thought for a moment, focusing on a cobweb in the corner of the landing ceiling. A fly was trapped in the intricate spool weaved by the tiny spider. Though to the fly, the spider was a monster.

A devil.

"His office," Swanson said. He turned to Aaron and the other officers. "Wait here."

He pushed past them all, but Hart followed close behind him. They went back down the stairs and into Randall's office. There were two officers already inside, who looked up from their rifling in surprise.

"Have you found any keys?" Swanson asked.

They looked around at each other and shook their heads. Swanson scanned the room. Where would that psycho hide keys? He went over to the desk and rummaged around the paperwork. Nothing.

He opened up the drawers and dug through the contents. But there was nothing other than paperwork and pens. Hart surveyed the shelves of books and boxes of paperwork, but she turned to him and shook her head.

He examined the room once more. It had to be in here somewhere. They were so close to finally accessing that damn third floor. Then his gaze landed on the bookshelf.
The Devil of Adrenna.
Bingo.

44

Swanson

Swanson's heart raced as he ran to the bookshelf and yanked *The Devil of Adrenna* off the shelf. He ripped it open and relief hit him. A rusted, bent key was sellotaped to the first page of the book. He peeled back the tape and released the key. It was heavy. Certainly a remnant of the asylum period. He held it up to Hart, and her face broke into a grin.

"Come on, let's find out all about that top floor," she said.

The pair raced back up the stairs to the top floor and pushed past the officers and Aaron, who had been standing in awkward silence judging from the relieved smile Aaron gave Swanson.

Swanson pushed the key into the lock and jiggled it to make it fit. Despite being bent out of shape, it turned, and the lock clicked open. He turned the handle with a shove and pushed open the bulky door. It was four inches thick, and creaked loudly as it opened. The nine of them stood still. No-one said a word.

The door opened up to a long corridor with a white-tiled

floor and one large window halfway down on the left-hand side. The first part of the corridor was gloomy, but the sun shone through the window and gave it an eerie light. Specks of dust floated in the sunlight. Two doors across from the window caught Swanson's attention but he stood rooted to the spot, lost in the feelings of wretchedness that escaped from the corridor.

Something was in that room, and he wasn't sure he wanted to know what it was.

And that was before the stench hit them. It snuck out as if trying to catch them unaware. Swanson held his arm up to his nose to block the foulness. Not that it was much use.

"Well, go on inside.' Hart's voice brought Swanson out of his reverie and he turned to glare at her before stepping forward into the sorrow. Slow footsteps followed him. No one was in a rush to be first.

"Er... I'm going to stay here." He heard Aaron's voice pipe up. "You know, to keep out of your way."

Swanson would have laughed, but he didn't blame him. A part of him wished he could stay outside, too. He'd had enough of creepy asylums. But he kept moving one foot in front of the other until he reached the window. He swiped away the dust in the air, which made no difference as the tiny particles continued to surround him as if trying to shoo him away.

He surveyed the car park below. This was the window he'd seen someone staring at them from. The deep burgundy curtain hung to one side now, but it had been closed. The face had disappeared behind it. Someone had been here since, and opened up the curtains fully.

"Holy hell, Swanson. Come look at this," Hart's yell cut through the thick atmosphere.

He turned and saw her standing a few feet behind him. She'd opened one door and was standing in the doorway staring into it. He walked over, and the scene took his breath away.

A winged statue of a creature he'd had never seen before stood in the middle of the room. Horns stuck out from the forehead and black staining mottled the grotesque face. It was positioned on top of a sort of unit with doors.

"I'm not going near that thing," Hart said with a look of disgust, "I'll wait here, go on boys."

She smirked as Swanson rolled his eyes and motioned for the other officers to follow him in.

"You can wait outside on your own," he said as he walked past her.

Her smirk dropped and she turned to look behind her. Swanson stepped over to the statue and ran a gloved finger across the face. It felt like stone under the rubber of the glove. He examined the dark, mottled parts, and a shiver ran through him as he realised it looked like old blood.

He moved his attention to the dark wooden cupboard underneath and opened up the door. It contained a few strange rocks and smaller statues, and a large, heavy book. He opened up the book and spotted an inscription written on the first page.

'The dogs always bark,
And the violets die a death,
When the Devil brings the dark,
And when he gets inside my head.

To the men lucky enough to be chosen to serve, may Satan be with you.'

His stomach felt cold. He flicked through the pages. It was all handwritten nonsense. He passed it to an officer to put it in a bag as evidence. Underneath the book was a pile of handwritten notes. More nonsense, probably. He picked them up. Not notes, letters. Letters to the devil. Each one was signed off by Billy Logan.

Swanson felt sick as he read through the letters. Letters written by his own doctor. Each one with detailed instructions on which women to kidnap.

Their names, addresses, jobs.

How to restrain them.

Where to take them so Tiffin could do the killing, apparently for the devil.

Randall really was only the servant. Tiffin was the real devil.

Swanson put them down and stepped out of the room. He needed to breathe. Hart still stood there, looking warily down the corridor.

"What? What did you find?"

He rubbed his face hard, as if trying to wipe away the memory of reading the letters. "Letters with detailed instructions on women to kidnap for Tiffin, or Billy, whatever the hell his name is."

Her face paled. "So there's more kidnapped women?"

"Dead women, probably. Not all of their addresses are Derby based."

"OK. And that smell?"

Swanson nodded down the hallway.

"Let's keep looking."

The pair kept their arms against their noses as they continued down the dim hallway. One more door lay at the end and from the vileness of the stink, they both knew there was only one thing it could be. They were still tentative as they made their way towards the door, and Swanson grimaced as he pushed it open.

The pair fell backwards as the stench hit them full pelt, gagging as they leant against the wall. Swanson's eyes streamed, but he turned to force himself to double check what he was calling in.

A room full of bone fragments and naked bodies. His eyes desperately searched for anyone that might be alive. But there were no signs of life. There were at least eight bodies in the room.

Here lay the women who were not good enough for the devil, Billy Logan.

45

Swanson

Swanson sat in his makeshift office, hiding from Murray. It was supposed to be his peaceful hideaway, but yet again Hart perched on the end of his desk.

"What a messed up family," she said slowly, staring off into space.

"Mmm," Swanson agreed, "you can see why Randall was drawn to Tiffin, and vice versa. It's a match made in heaven."

Her head snapped around. "Randall killed him!"

"Well, yes. Apart from that. That went wrong for him, didn't it? But that's what you get if you give someone as mentally disturbed as Randall drugs to enhance his visions. I mean, he might have been a doctor, but he wasn't the brightest spark, was he?"

She shuddered. "I know we shouldn't say it, but good riddance."

"Well, I wonder about Tiffin's family, though. What made him so messed up?"

"You've been spending too much time with Summer and her patients," Hart grinned, "how is she, anyway?"

"She's doing good. Should be out of hospital in a few days."

"And looking for a new job, I expect."

"Would you get a new job if a suspect stabbed you?"

"No, but I'm usually well surrounded by good guys. She's mostly surrounded by dangerous guys, and she has no backup. Hey, she should come work with us. Not long till she's a qualified forensic psychologist, right?"

Swanson raised an eyebrow. "True. Maybe she should."

"Well, just a thought. I'm going for food. Want anything?"

He shook his head and Hart walked off, finally leaving him with some peace to gather his thoughts. The dead bodies were being examined, and a few had matched up with missing women already. It appeared that Billy Logan had changed his name to Nick Tiffin not long after he'd punched Swanson in the face all those years ago. He'd finished medical school and became a doctor. A damn good one, apparently.

Until his urge reappeared, and he once again wanted Randall's help. Drugging Randall with small doses of LSD and telling him it would enable him to see the devil as he did. Not that Randall believed Swanson, yet. But maybe in time he would realise that Tiffin used him. One body had been a woman in her late forties to fifties named Brenda Randall. Swanson assumed that this was Randall's missing mother, murdered by her own son. And then there was Sally Tiffin, who was covered in bruises and scars from her husband, and had been glad to see him dead.

Hart's idea also played on his mind. Summer would make a great addition to the team as a profiler or something similar. She'd be safer and might enjoy it more. A smile spread across his lips as he thought about the pair of them working together, a plan already forming in his mind.

46

Summer

Summer couldn't remember the last time she'd been so excited. It had been two weeks to the day since Randall attacked her, and the hospital was finally allowing her home. Although she was under strict instructions to rest, a plethora of daily medication and no driving under any circumstances.

None of that mattered, though. She was finally to be reunited with Joshua.

He was waiting at home for her in their flat with her mum. Apparently, he was 'helping' to clean, which Summer had smiled at the thought of.

"You all good to get out of here?" Swanson asked her.

She patted the bag slung around her shoulder.

"Think so!"

"After you." He pointed at the exit.

"Don't think I won't be coming back here with you for your hospital appointment," she warned him.

"Yes, yes. I know," he muttered.

"I can't believe you left it to Hart to tell me."

"She's bloody telling everyone."

"Someone has to look after you and you're too stubborn to ask."

The pair walked out and into the busy corridor, dodging hospital beds and porters and busy nurses.

"Are you excited to be going home?" Swanson asked.

"Are you kidding! I feel like a kid at Christmas. I could even do a dance right here!"

He laughed. "Go on!"

She gave him a playful glance. "Maybe later."

Swanson stopped and turned to her. "What are you doing for dinner?"

"Oh," she paused and looked deep in thought, "I don't know. I haven't thought that far ahead."

"Well, it has to be a special one. Why don't you let me take you out if you're feeling up for it?"

"Oh, that would be lovely, but it's not that easy with Joshua."

"Bring him along. He knows we're friends. I'm sure he wouldn't think anything of it."

"Is it a dinner for friends?" She peered at him.

He cleared his throat, looking more nervous than usual. "Well, tonight, yes. But next weekend, maybe not?"

She nodded, but couldn't help her face breaking into a grin. "That sounds great."

"Excellent. So it's a date, finally."

She laughed and pushed his arm. He grabbed her arm and pulled her to him. She looked up at him, their eyes locked together.

"I sort of have a job offer for you," he said, "well, a career change."

Summer looked away and took a breath to calm her beating

heart. Jesus. Why on earth would he kiss her when she looked so awful? Greasy, matted hospital hair and pale as snow were not a good look. Although he asked her for dinner.

"Summer?" Swanson said with a laugh.

"Oh sorry, I was miles away. Yes? A job offer?"

"Yes. Come work with us once you're qualified. You can do profiling or intelligence. You'll be surrounded by good guys, always someone to help. It'll be safer."

She opened her mouth to laugh and refuse, but hesitated. It wasn't such a bad idea. Joshua had nearly lost his mum.

"I'll think about it," she replied as they walked off down the corridor together.

"You can let me know on our date next week," he said with a grin. She hadn't seen him grin like that before, ever. She had a feeling there was still a lot about Swanson she had left to learn.

And she was going to find out about it all.

Also by Ashley Beegan

The Holiday Home

The beautiful, old cottage in the Peak District was the perfect place for Simone to take a much-needed break following a horrific attack. Surrounded by nature and peace, she can finally relax.

Until she realises she isn't alone.

Her partner and therapist, Chris, insists there's nobody else there. She just needs to rest. But Simone finds out that this particular cabin has some dark secrets.

Secrets that people will kill to protect.

Printed in Great Britain
by Amazon